I0623167

A Secret Hope

A Goose Girl Retelling

Scarlett Luna Strange

Something Strange Publishing

A Note To Parents & What You'll Find In My Books

My Newsletter

Find My Books Here

Author's Note

Dearest Reader,

It is with great joy that I communicate to you that this author has chosen to write in British English rather than American English, as I am, simply put, not an American.

Thank you!

Dedicated to Mr. Alex.
A kinder man, I've never known
A sweeter soul, I've never met
You've accepted me
You've loved me
You're much older and wiser
And you're one of my dearest friends

Part One

A creature so pure

A servant so vile

A tale of mystery

Must transpire

For what comes next

May strike your heart

A story of love

Could fall apart

So wait once more

For the words to come

To find out next

What will be spun

Prologue

"**M**ama, please," I begged. "Don't make me go. I don't want to go." I held on to her as tightly as I could until there was no longer room for us to breathe. As my mother kissed me farewell and I watched the tears stream down her face, I knew my face reflected the same emotions.

I didn't want to be sent away from Maryn—my country, my home. I didn't want to end up in a new place with new rules and a new life. I didn't want foreign royalty to be watching over my shoulder, constantly wondering if I was going to make a mistake or ruin their whole country. I didn't want this drastic change.

But there was no role for me here. Our lands were already struggling, and the gold from the royals in Whyst would be more than enough to carry us through the drought we had faced for so long. I was to be their queen, and their gold was to be our saving grace.

"You can visit us," Enrich spoke softly as he crushed me to his chest. "You'll visit, I know you will, little sister."

"A visit could never be long enough." I sobbed into him. "What if something goes wrong? What if I need you? What if they hate me, and I can't learn their customs?"

He pulled away and held me at arm's length, peering down into my teary eyes. "Hush, Lina. You are a princess; you will be a queen. No one sane could ever hate you. You have always been our flawless, beautiful Lina, and that is who you shall remain."

"And, darling, we will write you," Mama cut in. "You will write us in return. It will be as though we are in the same room."

I glanced over at her and then back at Enrich before slowly nodding, trying to appear strong for them. "I purchased stationery here... in case theirs was not up to my standards."

"That was very wise." Enrich nodded, doting on me as usual. "I have also sent along as many familiar treats as I could, along with dried fruits from our orchard that they do not grow there."

I paused for a moment as his arms fell from mine. "What do you mean? Will the foods be so different?" Panic took over once more at the strange newness I was about to face.

"Calm down, calm down. You will not need to worry. There will be a crate sent every year with all the things you are accustomed to. You need not change your preferences if you do not wish to."

Taking a deep breath, I took in my surroundings. The glass hall I would no longer see that brought so much light to my life. The flowers that filled the vases next to the thrones. The mural painted onto the glass ceiling above me, a mosaic of colour and light showcasing a rainbow whenever the sun reflected onto it. I didn't know when, or if, I would see this room again.

"Lina, it is time," Mama reminded me gently.

I nodded, fighting back tears once more. I knew it was time. I knew this was when it would all truly begin for me.

"You'll have Grendy. She has always been a loyal maid to you, and I know she will continue to be," Mama reminded me. "Lean on her, and she will guide you through this journey."

"Indeed, Princess Catalina," Grendy offered a gracious bow from her place behind me. "You can always rely on me. We will enter this new land together."

With one last hug to my mother and a kiss pressed to my temple from my brother, I turned to face the future. I had no idea what was coming, but I knew they were right.

This dowry would save our land. This marriage would give us two kingdoms. And I could always count on Grendy.

Chapter One

Catalina

My tears continued to fall as I sat in the coach, the jostling ride making my heart jump. I watched out the window as the countryside passed by faster than I would like it to, and all I could do was feel sorry for myself.

This was a truly horrible time in my life, and I would never think of it as anything but the worst day in existence.

What if I never saw these lands again? What if this final memory would be all I had for the rest of my time spent living? I couldn't stand the agony I felt as everything around me changed forever.

Grendy gave a small cough, her usual way of getting my attention, and I turned to her. "Princess, we will be nearing our first stop soon. Perhaps you'd like to go over the plans for this trip?"

Trust her to always distract me when I needed it most. There would never be anyone I could rely on more than dear Grendy.

"Yes," I sputtered, hating how shaky and weak my voice sounded from crying. "I suppose that would be wise. I cannot recall where we will be stopping, or even how long the journey is."

I couldn't interpret the smile she gave, but her chuckle told me enough. At times, I wondered if she thought me a spoiled young woman, but if she did, she never let on. "There is a parchment in your clutch where I have placed our itinerary."

"Oh, you truly are the most organized person I have ever met." I felt relieved that I would require little brain space to go over the journey. Opening the clutch next to me, I pulled out the parchment she had mentioned.

I untied the string holding it closed and unrolled it, reading over the words slowly so I could better prepare myself. The thought of this being required at all made me want to throw it out the window. But, letting out a sigh, I knew such childish antics were behind me.

The page was filled with places I knew nothing about. Unfamiliar names were underlined, and some were circled. She had taken the liberty of writing notes about each place, as well as the pronunciation, if it was needed.

"There are some places we will be stopped at to replenish our supplies—those are the ones you see circled. We are going far from these lands and the languages will differ. A translator will meet us in these ports, but I've included pronunciations for key phrases so as not to offend."

I marveled at her diligence and gave her a nod. "Yes. This is perfect, Grendy. Thank you for taking the time to do this. It will be most helpful."

There was no verbal response to my praises; Grendy merely nodded as she gestured for me to continue my overview of her work.

The timeline of our journey wasn't as long as most I had heard about and for that, I was grateful. We would spend about a month aboard this ship and see Whyst by mid-summer. This was a journey that could only be made this time of year as our harbour froze from late fall to mid-spring. The last had thawed, and we could now make the ride across our oceans.

There was fear creeping in as I once again realized I wasn't just going to a kingdom that was near ours. This was no neighbouring land of a kingdom we had an alliance with; this was a land so far away, in such an unfamiliar place, that even in my upbringing with my extensive studies, I had not learned of it.

It was not until our counsel had extended our reaches and sent diplomats out to further our knowledge that we learned about Whyst and the riches they had to offer. This marriage was the result of three years of trips and planning.

So, when my brother spoke of my visiting home in the future, I knew we both felt it was unlikely. Once I was in Whyst, I would likely remain there and only see their neighbouring countries. I would forever be away from our lands.

"Princess, your face will wrinkle permanently if you do nothing to stop those tears." Grendy's soft voice chided, and I couldn't resist the giggle that escaped me.

"You're right, and a wrinkled face will do nothing to endear me to a king." I sniffled. I reached out and grasped the handkerchief she offered before adding, "A king I do not even know... one I have never met."

Her eyes did not meet mine, and I knew what that meant—she was also wary of this unknown king, one who had only been met through diplomats. While my brother and the king had corresponded about our union, there had never been any introduction. I was going into this blind.

I couldn't hide the fear that constantly wove through me, as though creating a tapestry I would never be able to shed. There would never be any escape for me once we were wed.

"Now, now, princess," Grendy spoke up, her light accent lilting. "It won't be so bad. Your brother would never send you to a man he was not sure of."

She was right, but there was something in her eyes I couldn't read. Almost as though she couldn't quite convince herself of this fact.

"What is it, Grendy? What are you trying not to tell me?" I probed.

"Ah, I shouldn't say... it wouldn't be right." Her face turned to the window, but I couldn't look away from her. "Only..."

"Only what?" Oh, why couldn't she just spit it out? My thoughts wouldn't rest until I knew exactly what was running through her mind.

"It's nothing, princess." She paused. "Only, I find it strange that a brother would not journey with his sister to make an introduction or see the land with his own eyes... to assure himself of her safety."

Her words confirmed my deepest fears. She was right; Enrich had done no such thing. He couldn't fully know where I would end up or what kind of man this king would be. But it was much too late to change anything now. I was trapped.

"I apologize if I caused alarm," she added hastily. "I'm sure your brother knows what he is doing. I, myself, am not familiar with these royal matters."

I heard the driver call out to the horses, and our coach came to a halt. We had reached our first stop and would remain here for the night before continuing to reach the harbour tomorrow.

Despite the exhaustion of a day spent on the road, my mind could not stop spinning. Grendy was right. There was no telling what position my brother had placed me in. The fear and resistance in my heart tightened, and I knew there would be no sleep tonight.

Chapter Two

Catalina

I tried to reason with myself over and over again as I lay in bed that night. It wasn't the bed's scratchy linens or Grendy's soft snores in the corner, nor was it the guard stationed by the window or the one outside my door, that kept me awake that night.

Enrich couldn't very well leave the kingdom just like that. He was to be the king—although, he wasn't the king yet. As long as Mama lived, he was the prince. True, he had arranged this marriage and was in charge of most duties, but in title, Mama was the ruler of the country.

He could have traveled with me, and Mama would have been fine to run things, just as they had always been. Or if he was concerned with leaving her alone, there was nothing stopping him from venturing out in the recent years without me.

Why did he not do such a thing, then? Gone on his own journey and returned, sure of himself and his decision. Instead of using diplomats and messengers before sending his very own sister out to a fate he had no idea of.

I turned for what felt like the millionth time that night and let out a sigh. This wouldn't do. I knew my spoiled side was beginning to show, and that I had very little to complain about in the grand scheme of things.

If Enrich had traveled and something happened to him, I'd still be in the same position of needing to wed. I would have been able to remain in my own kingdom, but a stranger would be my husband in that situation as well.

Logically, this was the only solution that would truly benefit the kingdom of Maryn. This way, a king remained in the country and a princess could solidify an alliance, initiate a trade route, and refill the royal coffers. This marriage set our country up for success in a way we could only dream of.

Enrich had said we were likely exhausting the resources of our neighbouring lands. Not to mention, we could scarcely afford to keep purchasing resources from Zenyth. They had been nothing but kind; however, they had their own to look after as well.

Even as I wracked my mind, attempting to think of a solution, I knew none could be found. I knew it was likely a night such as this that Enrich had faced as he made the difficult decisions that were required of a king.

Yet, despite the logic I kept pushing my mind to follow along with, the panicked spiral continued. Nothing could change the fact that I was walking into a terrifying situation that couldn't be prevented, no matter how hard I tried.

If it could be prevented, would I take a way out? The question made me sit upright in my bed, startling the guard by my window.

"Princess?" he questioned awkwardly, unused to situations such as this. "Have you heard something? Are you alarmed?"

I waved my hand and collapsed back down to stare at the ceiling. "No, no. Nothing. Merely a dream. Thank you."

No, not a dream; a nightmare. This was all shaping up to be one big nightmare. And I felt as if I would never wake up.

Chapter Three

Catalina

"Good morning, princess," Grendy greeted me, enthusiastic as ever, a large smile painting her face. "Was the bed to your liking? Did you rest well?"

I would have loved to give a snarky answer, but the manners I was raised with never allowed that, so all I could manage was, "Everything was satisfactory." I knew my expression betrayed the words, but neither of us commented on that.

"Wonderful," she stated. "We'll need to eat quickly if we're to leave on time. I've already sent for breakfast to be brought here. It would be best to avoid eating in the dining room."

Her familiar nose wrinkle was always a comical sight to me. Despite being my lady's maid, Grendy had more royal pride than even my mother did. She felt it was beneath me to be eating in a common space like the dining room of a traveler's inn, and I knew better than to disagree.

"Although…" She spoke up once more before trailing off for a moment. "I do hope the fare is good enough. This was the only place we could stop at, and while I searched for another, the best one was out of the way by at least an hour. Your mother did not approve it."

I hid the smile behind my hands, but I could very well picture Mama rolling her eyes at Grendy's aversion to the less finer things in life. "I'm sure this will be more than adequate."

A knock sounded at the door, and she rushed to answer it. Opening the door wide, she instructed the tavern maid to set our breakfast on the small table next to the window. My stomach growled, likely as a result of the tossing and turning I'd experienced at night.

The tray had croissants, muffins, fruits, sausages, and eggs. There was more than we could ever finish, but I knew this was the royal treatment I should have expected. The maid exited in a hurry, and Grendy turned to look over the food piled before us.

She gave a swift nod in my direction. "I suppose this will do."

With relief, I sat down and began to move generous servings of everything onto my plate. A raised eyebrow from Grendy wasn't enough to slow me down this morning.

Between bites of a blueberry muffin, she cleared her throat, and I looked up. "I'll begin the review of our itinerary for the day," she began.

Not even my breakfast would be enjoyed in peace. Grendy would not waste a minute of time that could be spent in productivity. It was almost enough to make me rethink having her along for the trip. But I quickly dismissed that and did what I could to tolerate this moment.

"Our next leg of the journey will take us the last nine hours to the harbour. We will stop every two hours for fifteen minutes, including an hour-long lunch. We'll have a respite for sandwiches as our dinner, and then dine fully at the harbour."

I nodded, filling my mouth with the delicious breakfast as she rambled. I already had been briefed on these things before leaving, but I supposed it was as good a reminder as any.

"We will stay the night in an inn by the harbour, where we will also have breakfast before boarding the ship and setting sail." She finally looked up and placed the paper down, choosing a few breakfast items for her plate.

"Thank you, Grendy. It seems we are well prepared for our journey."

"Yes," she replied. "But tell me, how are you feeling about this all? I worry for you, princess. A long trip to a strange new land can be difficult."

I hesitated at her question. I knew I could trust her with how I felt, it wasn't that. I just knew expressing anything wouldn't change my situation. Wrestling with Mama's approval in my mind, I gave my best smile. "It is new, to be sure, but I know my family would only send me somewhere they truly felt was right for me."

Honestly, I didn't know that for sure, given Grendy's words last night. It wasn't like me to doubt my brother doing his due diligence—I always had faith in him and his abilities—yet here I was, shaken by what Grendy had brought up, only out of concern in her kind heart.

"Well, as long as you're feeling comfortable and at ease, that is all that matters." She chattered happily, smearing butter onto a halved croissant. "Besides, lots of women marry complete strangers and hardly any of them end up in harm's way. You're sure to be one of the lucky ones."

She kept speaking, but my heart froze at her words. I hadn't considered the fact that I could be marrying a monster. Of course, I had thought about marrying a stranger—that thought never left my mind. But somehow, I had been operating under the assumption that I would be received by a handsome, kind king. As though this was a fact. Yet, I didn't know it to be true. I had so very little information to go on when it came to this man.

I looked over at Grendy and felt a flash of envy. Yes, she was my maid, and she was dedicating her life to serving me, but she had freedom I could only dream of. On her days off, she wandered around the nearby villages, visited family and friends, chose whether to marry or not, and at the age of twenty-two, had seen more of Maryn than I had. I envied her life.

I would trade places with her in a heartbeat if I could.

"Princess?" Grendy's furrowed brows watched me from across the table. "I'm sure the king will enjoy this daydreaming habit of yours," she pointed out with a chuckle. "But you really should finish your breakfast."

The hunger I had felt earlier seemed to disappear, but I reached down to make some progress on the scrambled eggs that were still steaming on my plate. Perhaps I should pour my heart out to Grendy on our upcoming carriage ride. I'm sure, given her own voiced concerns, she would empathize with mine.

Deciding to do just that, I did what I could to swallow every last bite.

Chapter Four

Catalina

T he carriage jostled as we rode through the various towns that dotted our journey. I hadn't found the nerve to speak to Grendy yet, but I felt as though she knew I had something to say. I was not someone who could so easily hide my emotions, and she could read me like a book.

"Grendy, I wondered if we might speak." I finally managed the words, and she laid down the book she had been reading since our last stop. "About some personal matters."

"Of course, princess." She smiled endearingly as she gestured with her free hand to continue. "Whatever you would like to share."

"I find myself out of sorts," I began, then paused, unsure of how to continue. Taking a deep breath, I knew there was no other way to put it. "I do have many concerns about marrying an unknown man and living in this new kingdom. It isn't that I don't trust my family or their decisions. It's only that…"

She was nodding as I spoke in an effort to encourage me, and I found the courage to continue, "Sometimes I just wonder what it would be like to have another choice, another option. To be someone else."

I couldn't meet her gaze as I knew the incredible privilege I had in my family. I was taking it for granted with someone who likely longed to have what I had.

"I wouldn't wish for your life, princess."

My eyes whipped back to meet hers and I felt shocked. I knew I had envied her life, but I had always assumed she envied mine, given her ability to put on airs and assume more than she should. Yet, it didn't seem like that at all when I looked at her now.

"That isn't to say I don't appreciate the life you live or the work it affords me," she rushed to fill the shocked silence. "I only mean to say that, being in your position would terrify me to my core. You are very brave."

I couldn't resist the smile at her easy compliment, but there was so much I had left unsaid. I didn't want her to think I was complaining, but I was also dying to lay my soul bare.

"Grendy," I took a deep breath, "have you ever wanted to trade places before?"

She blinked at me as though her eyes were processing what my mouth was saying. "I'm not sure I follow, princess."

"Never mind." I was quick to brush it off, as it was likely just a silly thought, but I saw her expression change and, for a moment, I wanted to press the issue.

"No, no. Please. I would love to hear your thoughts some more."

With a quick smile that I hoped showed some kind of humour, I let out a short laugh. "It's silly, but sometimes I wonder what it would be like to be you. I know it is not glamorous, and you work so very hard, but I suppose it's hard not to wonder."

I was expecting her to be offended or outright appalled that a princess would want to be a maid, but instead, she nodded slowly. "It's easy to wonder what someone else's life is like."

I let out a sigh and a shaky laugh. "I'm relieved you think so. I have so many hesitations now that we are on the road to Whyst. Almost as though I've changed my mind, though I'm not at liberty to do that."

"You might not be able to change your mind, but maybe... No, no, that's too ridiculous."

"What?" I questioned, moving forward in my seat in the carriage. "What were you going to say?"

"Forget I said anything, princess; it's too ridiculous for words." Her eyes moved back to the landscape we passed, and I knew I was running out of time. We could already hear the sounds of the gulls singing near the harbour, and I had to know where she was going with this.

"Please, say it."

Grendy turned back to me and leaned in as though someone could overhear us. "I was just thinking how fun it would be to trade places with you for a while. But it's a crazy idea and, of course, it would never work."

She had said it so flippantly, but I couldn't help but latch onto the idea. It was a crazy one, as she said, but oh, it was tempting. I so badly wanted to just throw caution to the wind and grasp onto anything that would change this fate of mine.

"It could work," I whispered to her.

With eyes wider than a saucer, her mouth fell open. "You can't be serious."

"Why not?" I questioned.

"Because... Well... How would we manage that?" she sputtered. "We would need months of careful planning and work in order to execute that well."

"Grendy, you and I have been together for so long, we practically sing in harmony. All we would need is a night to come up with our plan, and then it would be simple," I insisted. "We could trade places; you could figure out who the king is, and if it goes well, we'll switch back as though it was a simple practical joke, and it'll be done!"

Her hesitation was more than I could bear, and I could hear the voices calling for us to halt outside our final stop. We had reached the inn where we would dine and spend the night, but I desperately longed for an answer from her. Something that would tell me there was a way around this mess. It was a flawed plan already, but there had to be something I could do.

"Okay, princess," was all she said.

"Really?" I questioned, wanting to make sure I had heard her right.

"Let's do it."

Chapter Five

Catalina

"All aboard and ready to sail!" the shipmate called out as a horn blast sounded in the air.

We had been seated on this vessel for only half an hour and already, my stomach felt as though it was turning an uncomfortable amount. Could I truly last for an entire month at sea? The summer air was warm, and I breathed a sigh of relief when the cool ocean breeze hit me.

Grendy was managing fine and had been walking around the deck without a care in the world. Great. Yet another thing to envy her for. She was completely at ease, laughing at the crew's jokes and looking out across the vast ocean that lay before us.

"Gre—" I cut myself off before I fully slipped up. "Princess," I corrected. "Would you not like to sit down for a moment as our journey begins?"

She cast a smile in my direction and flipped her head as a gust of wind blew her blonde curls around—curls we had spent all morning arranging so they would fall perfectly, as any princess's would.

With a short walk over to me, she sat, and we nodded to a passerby. Leaning over to me, she whispered, "This is going very well so far."

I couldn't resist the laugh that escaped before my own whispered response, "We've only just begun and have kept it up for merely half an hour. Were you under the impression we would slip up sooner?"

"Honestly, I wasn't sure what to expect. But we have managed quite well."

Last night, I had practically forced the guard to leave my room—pleading some feminine condition that embarrassed him far too much to ask questions—and requested he stand guard below the window outside instead.

We had spent hours poring over notes I had created for Grendy over supper and quizzing her on everything she needed to know before we boarded the ship. We had a month before our arrival in Whyst, but that didn't mean we had much time alone during that month. The princess would be under closer guard than ever during this journey, and we couldn't afford to take chances on messing up.

The trickiest part would be the changing of the guard. There were a few my brother had personally met with while looking over the treaty, and while I didn't meet any of them, we had to make sure every description matched what he said exactly.

My guards would hand me over to Whyst's guards before we boarded, and then it was up to Grendy and me to somehow make the transition between each other.

The weather was on our side, as a cold breeze meant we didn't need an excuse to wear our black cloaks. We were able to easily switch positions as we walked up the plank, with one of us bending to fetch a dropped handkerchief and seamlessly blending together after.

I was shocked by how smoothly it had gone and, at Grendy's request to be escorted to her chamber immediately for a refresh prior to sailing, we made our switch official. She had already been wearing my shoes and now we made quick work of trading dresses, placing my gold tiara on her blonde curled hair.

My own hair was curly by nature, but Grendy styled it back as hers often was, in a bun at the nape of her neck, and no one was the wiser.

Yes, our switch had gone over smoother than either of us had expected, and I was filled with relief. Hopefully, we could relax now. The guards had been changed and there was no one aboard who would recognize me for who I was. I was finally living in anonymity.

"Now, behind closed doors, we must not let our act fall apart," I insisted for the millionth time as I unpacked. "Everything must be exactly the way it is out there."

She nodded and gave me a quick smile. "Yes, Prin— Grendy," she swiftly corrected.

It was much easier for us to stay the course if we made sure to keep everything the exact same, whether we were out on a stroll or here in our own beds.

"You just never know who will come barreling through that door."

"Come now. You're sounding awfully paranoid," the maid-turned-princess responded. "No one would barge in when it comes to royalty. There will always be a respectful knock first. Always."

The door swung open and we jumped, turning to see who the intruder was. A hand was raised as though to knock, and there was a shocked man standing before us, instantly apologetic.

"I beg your pardon," he gasped. "I was merely coming to introduce myself and this door flew right open!"

Grendy and I looked at each other and couldn't stifle the giggles that escaped us. "My good sir," Grendy choked out through her laughter, "would you find a handyman to come and secure this door for us? It simply wouldn't be proper to have it fly open at the slightest gust of wind."

The man turned red as a ripe apple and stammered his apologies, insisting he would fetch someone at once, before practically running away.

We collapsed onto our beds, the humour still washing over us. This was sure to be an entertaining month at sea.

Chapter Six

Catalina

The first dinner aboard the ship was an interesting one. It was clear that the captain had told his men to be on their best behaviour. Everyone came so dressed up, it was shocking to see. He presented his main men and informed us we would see them about the ships, and his only request would be to steer clear of those who were on shift.

We had free rein on the boat—other than the mechanical room—and I may have indulged in the kitchen already on the first day. I had longed to learn the art of cooking and practically begged the cook for a chance to learn during our journey.

She had looked at me warily. "Aren't you the maid to the princess?"

"Yes, but she naps every afternoon, and I'm certain I could come down and help prepare supper when the time comes. Please?"

Eventually, she relented, if only to get rid of me. So not only would I be enjoying my first free vacation from royal life, but I could finally learn a skill I had been jealous of for over a decade. It was simply too good to be true!

"Ah, Grendy," Grendy leaned in to nudge me, "you must assist me in seating. I am not accustomed to it in such an elaborate gown. Please." Her expression pleaded with me for some help.

While I was wearing her simpler dresses, poor Grendy was stuck wearing the elaborate gowns that showcased my family's culture and beauty. They were not of the most comfortable variety, and while I would have thrown them overboard were I forced into them for this journey, I knew Grendy was much more proper than I was.

"Yes, of course." I rushed out, leaning over to hold her gown and adjust it around her as she seated herself. After even one day in her dresses, I wasn't sure I could ever wear one of my old gowns again. I had heard the fashion in Whyst was much more toned down, and that was something I could adjust to.

As I sat in my place next to her, I glanced at the portion that sat before me. While it was not the delectable food I was used to back home, the fresh sea air had already increased my appetite, and it was all I could do to keep my manners.

One glance at Grendy told me she was less than impressed. "So this is to be our fare as we travel?" Her nose wrinkled as the smell of spices hit her, and she turned to me, one eyebrow raised.

I was quick to reassure her. "Don't worry, I'm sure I can persuade the cook to create some dishes from home."

"And how will you manage that?"

"I've secured a time every afternoon to learn how to cook."
If I could only sketch the expression that looked back at me—a
face of pure shock. She lost some of her proper posture as she
blinked.

"Why on earth would you want to spend your time learning
such a thing?"

"I've always wanted to learn. Of course, given my prior situation, it was never something that was considered." I couldn't
read the expression in Grendy's eyes, but what I could interpret
outside of the shock was that she was impressed.

"I suppose I never considered you to have interests outside
of..."

"Drawing, embroidery, and riding?" I spoke quietly, listing
the top accomplishments that were required of a lady at court.
"I suppose they were never worth mentioning, given I'd never
have the chance to pursue other interests. Now, thanks to you,
I have that chance."

I saw a look of regret in her eyes, but it was so fleeting, I was
sure I was mistaken. She nodded and the man on her opposite
side leaned over, catching her attention.

Truthfully, I'd never eaten in such silence before. Every
word, every glance, everything was directed toward Grendy. She
looked truly exhausted by the time dessert came around, and I
had scarcely spoken two words to a single soul at our table. This
was what it felt like to be an overlooked maid.

"And what was your name again?"

I had nearly completed my first supper on this ship without addressing anyone, so when a question did eventually come my way, all I could do was stare. It was the man who had nearly knocked on our door earlier. Frankly, I hadn't even noticed he was my table companion until now.

It surprised me that I had missed him, given the dark hair and eyes that were now looking in my direction. He was handsome, although not the sort I would usually notice. No, my companions were generally well-dressed gentry, not sailors in their rustic best.

"If you'd please…" he requested at my silence.

"Grendy. My name is Grendy," I replied with a smile on my face, my hand raising a spoon of chocolate pudding. I was already good at assuming the name.

"Welcome, Grendy. I apologize again for my earlier mishap. The door to your room has had new hinges put on, so it won't be happening again."

I giggled at that, and his cheeks tinged red. "The princess and I were thankful for the entertainment you provided us. I'm sure it will not be the only comical incident we share."

There was a brief smirk across his handsome face, and he gave a slight bow of his head. "I'm pleased to be of service to you both."

"And your name was?"

"Alion," he replied quickly. "Ship's mate and a lover of good food." He raised the glass of wine at the table in my direction and gave a quick wink.

Yes, I could see this journey passing very pleasantly indeed.

Chapter Seven

Catalina

I always felt like a month was something that dragged on, given how nothing ever changed back at court, but this month, on board a ship, was passing much faster than I would have liked. Every day held a new adventure for me as I learned how the ship worked and watched as the chef cooked. Grendy had given me the gift of freedom in a way I never knew was possible.

One day I was learning how to whip up stew with biscuits; the next, I was learning how to tie knots. My previous dull life had changed into something fast-paced, busy, and exciting.

Of course, there wasn't too much bragging I wanted to do where Grendy was concerned, as I could already see the life of a princess wearing on her. The bags under her eyes showed how little she slept, the clothing that limited her movements so drastically, the constant need to be on her best behaviour. She was not thriving as I was. Life at sea under constant supervision did not suit her.

She rarely complained to me at the end of the day, and while that was curious to me, she seemed hesitant to voice anything these days. I tried to engage her in conversation, but she would always respond with how tired she felt, how long her day had been.

We were nearing the third week of our voyage before she finally said something.

"You never mentioned the exhaustion that takes over from always being... on," she finished lamely.

I was pulling on my nightdress and gave her a halfhearted smile. "I guess it's not something I ever thought about, given how it was just expected of me."

She nodded and sat on her bed, looking over at me, watching my expression closer than I would have liked. "Do you notice it more now? Given the freedom you've had a taste of these days?"

I thought for a moment, not wanting to rub in what a fantastic time I was having as she struggled. "I do. Life feels lighter and, if I'm honest, I would love nothing more than to never step foot in a palace again. I love the feeling of falling into bed after a day's work. Being a princess has many challenges and it is hard work, but it is different. The load is more mental, more emotional. This is different."

It was hard to communicate exactly what I meant, but she seemed to understand. "I would agree with you there. The life of a maid is more physically taxing, and you've also been applying yourself as we sail, which is admirable."

"Do you regret changing places? Because we could cut our little joke off early and change back."

"No!" She jumped up, startling me. "No." There was hesitation in her voice, and she quickly looked around our room. "I will manage. We are nearly complete with our voyage, and I'm sure once we enter the king's palace, all will be different. I will have more to occupy my time, and you will have some digging to do about your betrothed."

Her reaction was a strange one, but there wasn't much I could do. She was right, of course; we couldn't stop now, not when we were so much closer to our original goal. Besides, I was enjoying my time being just a maid. There was so much left for me to learn.

"Tomorrow I'm learning how to dress a chicken," I brought up out of nowhere in an effort to ease the awkwardness in the room. "We plucked the feathers today, actually. It was quite an exciting experience."

Grendy's nose wrinkled in disgust as she flashed me a quick smile. "You're a strange one, princess. A very strange one."

"I know."

It turned out dressing a chicken was not something I was good at. In fact, I wasn't good at anything involving chicken. It turned out, the raw bird held little appeal as I touched it, with my mind only focusing on how slimy it felt.

Chicken pie. Chicken fried. Chicken soup. Cream of chicken. Roast chicken.

Indeed, how could there be so many meals I loved that focused on this bird, when seeing it raw made me want to vomit?

"You're looking a little green there, Miss."

I turned to face the laughing face of Alion, who couldn't contain his mirth. Leave it to this man to find me at my absolute worst every single time. It wasn't enough that he'd seen me hanging by my wrist when I knotted my own hand to the mainmast. Or that he'd been the one to change out the bucket during my first moments at sea. And I couldn't forget the unfortunate moment when a wave drenched me while I assisted in pulling in the nets, and he got a decent look at the lucky green tights I always snuck on under my dresses.

This man had exceptionally bad timing, and it made me want to clock him on the head. But one look at that grin and even I had to admit, there was no being angry with this man.

With a sigh, I waved him over to stand next to me. "Learning to cook isn't easy. I'd thank you to remember that."

A smirk lit his face. "I wouldn't know. I've never cooked a day in my life. And it baffles me that you'd want to learn. Isn't that what living in your palace is for?"

I froze for a moment. *Living in my palace?* What was he hinting at?

He must have noted my response as the smile slipped. "Do the maids not get cooked for in your position? I assumed, since you wait on the princess, that your main focus is her."

I let out a breath of relief. He had no idea. I was being silly. Of course he didn't know. We hadn't slipped up, and we'd done exceptionally well with our secret.

"You're right. I do enjoy some fine dining and have never cooked prior to this. But I am always willing to learn a new skill, especially one as necessary as cooking."

"Well, alright then." Alion began rolling up his sleeves.

"What are you doing?" I questioned in confusion.

"Learning how to dress a chicken."

Chapter Eight

Catalina

It was a windy day in Whyst when we at long last arrived. Grendy had grown weary of ship life and, despite my best efforts, nothing seemed to pull her out of the place in her mind she had traveled into these last few weeks. It was almost as though we were no longer as close as we had been, but that had to be my imagination. The journey was wearing on her, that's all it was.

As I laced up my gown—as I had gotten into the habit of doing myself—and turned to help Grendy, I found she was staring into the mirror, gone from our world.

"Grendy?" I spoke up hesitantly. "Are you quite well?"

Her eyes flashed to mine in the reflection, a guarded expression on her face. "Of course, princess. We've finally arrived, and I can leave this dreaded ship. I was only thinking..."

I knew that process all too well. She was always hesitant to share her thoughts with me, despite the fact that we'd been living in close quarters and had already changed places. Why was there always a pause from her?"If you have thoughts to share, please do so. You know I've always allowed us to speak freely with one another."

She nodded and turned to face me. "I know we intend to keep this ruse up until we have more information, but I saw how much you've enjoyed yourself, and I wondered if you might like more freedom than you would find inside the palace walls. It's not the same as being on a ship."

I blinked at her in confusion. "More freedom? What did you have in mind?"

"Well..." Grendy looked around the room as though someone was hiding behind a curtain, "there is a field not far from the palace walls. One of the ship's mates has family there who runs a goose farm."

"A goose farm... What on earth is the purpose of—"

"I asked the same question," she cut me off with a giggle. "They couldn't even come up with a response other than for food. One certainly cannot milk a goose, and there are no eggs made of gold."

"What were you thinking?" I spoke up before silence could follow her words.

A knock on the door startled us, and I rushed to open it, eager to send the person away and get to the bottom of Grendy's long train of thought. Flinging the door wide, I found Alion's chipper face on the other end. I swallowed a groan. While I had gotten to know him well this past month, his presence had begun to grate on me. His eagerness, his ready smile, the attitude that never seemed shaken or even remotely temperamental. Was it possible for someone to be too happy? Because he constantly was.

"We're about ready to lower the walkway so we can head onto land. I expect you're both nearly ready to depart the ship?"

"I am," Grendy moaned, before freezing and sputtering, "I mean, I would enjoy land... Not that a ship isn't fun, it's only—"

Alion laughed in good humour, as he always did. "Worry not, princess. I know sea life has not been kind to you. I look forward to my time on land as well." He looked at her closely as he spoke, and I raised an eyebrow in his direction. What was he trying to figure out about her? Surely, he hadn't sorted out our secret. It couldn't be...

"Alion, can you leave?" I spoke up bluntly. Thankfully, being a maid had given me certain liberties in how I addressed others. While Grendy had to pull back and bite her tongue, I was given free rein to say whatever I'd like.

"Pri— Grendy!" Grendy gasped. "Do not be rude. He was merely checking up on us to make sure our affairs were in order."

I smirked at her nearly slipping up, and glanced at Alion. "The princess and I really must see to a discussion you interrupted. We will be along shortly. Thank you." Closing the door in his face, I turned to Grendy to find her eyes narrowed in my direction.

"Princess," she started in a hushed whisper, "you will need to learn your manners anew once you take up your position again."

I waved my hand in annoyance. "Never mind that. What were you saying earlier? About geese?"

A ready smile lit her face as though she had not just been lamenting about her time at sea. "How would you like to try your hand at being a goose girl? The field is a short walk from the palace, and we can run back and forth at night to exchange information."

Words poured out of her mouth in excitement as my mouth fell open. It was one thing to live on a closed-in ship and enjoy the freedom from the safety onboard, but to be completely on my own out there? Where would I live? What would I be doing, other than minding... geese?

Her voice kept on, as though she hadn't noticed my expression. "You could get to know the surrounding villages, and everything would be open to you without the pompousness of royalty getting in the way. Everyone would share with you and—"

My mind had whisked me away before she even finished speaking. She had a good point. As a regular old goose girl, I could spend my days wandering around the villages, tending to geese and listening to the locals talk and the children play. I could experience more than just four closed walls in a palace.

It wouldn't be forever, and once I grew weary of that life, I could always trade back. It wasn't as though I needed to remain trapped as a goose girl forever.

"Of course…" Grendy's voice brought me back to the cramped room we'd spent this month in. "I can't imagine the king would take kindly to his betrothed's maid working out in a field."

"What do you mean?"

"Well, we don't know him," she pointed out. "Is he a snob? If so, he wouldn't very well want his queen's maid to be a goose girl. And then to later find out, the goose girl was his betrothed all along… But what could we do?"

An idea came to mind. "I could sneak out now, before anyone's the wiser. No one would need to know. If the ship's crew questions my whereabouts, you could say I'd disembarked earlier. If the king questions where your maid was, you could explain she was homesick and request a new attendant from his court."

Grendy's eyes glowed brighter as I shared my thoughts. "Princess," she whispered. "That's perfect. And when all is said and done, we merely claim I was sent ahead to test the waters and you followed closely behind. I see no flaws in this plan. It isn't as though the crew is in direct conversation with the king…"

Our voices rose in excitement as the plans continued to flow. With a new excitement in our steps, we prepared for my early departure.

Chapter Nine

Catalina

The rush of leaving the ship in secret was a thrilling endeavor. I was shoving things into a pack as quickly as I could. We were to dock in less than twenty minutes, and I couldn't afford to waste time.

"Don't forget to take coin for your needs. You won't be paid for some time, and the position of a goose girl likely doesn't provide much," Grendy reminded me, always thinking of everything. "I'll visit you twice a week, but only at night, and I'm not sure what I can get to you without anyone noticing."

We both giggled at the thought of sneaking around after all the deception we had already played at during our journey on this ship.

I don't think Grendy understood the magnitude of the gift she was giving me. Freedom to do whatever I pleased on this ship, along with freedom outside of the palace walls in the land I'd call my own. I felt much more comfortable doing these things than just being thrown into a palace, marrying a king, and ruling a country.

It felt strange preparing for yet another change, but my heart was fluttering with excitement. This was truly a brilliant idea, and no one could fault us for being cautious when it came to the king. We really didn't know what he was like, so it was safer having Grendy act as my decoy and report back to me.

We left the room, and I walked farther behind Grendy. Sticking to the shadows would be wiser as we weren't sure who was below deck to watch our interesting parade. It would be tricky sneaking me off a ship that had a crew this bustling, but it needed to be done in order to make it work.

I had dressed in a pair of sailor's bottoms we'd found hanging on a line. With my hair shoved under a cap and a jacket hiding my figure, we made our way above with Grendy keeping a sharp lookout.

Thankfully, we attracted little notice, as everyone was too busy preparing to land. I was able to slip in with a group of sailors who were eager to be the first off and gave Grendy a short wave. We'd make it so far, but here's hoping I could really escape notice.

I kept my head down and gave the occasional gruff laugh when comments were made. The sailors talked about what they most looked forward to when docking. Dinner with their favourite girl, a visit to see their parents, and endless food that didn't smell of sailors, stale biscuits, and ale. I'd take offense to the stale biscuits, but it was true. Rations had been of lesser quality near the end of our journey.

After what felt like forever, it was finally time to walk down the long plank to land. My legs were wobbly as I stepped onto the dock.

"Aye, lad, be careful," a lilting voice called out with a laugh. "Your sea legs need a moment to feel land. First sail is always the hardest."

I deepened my voice and thanked him before walking to a crowded area. This must be the group waiting for whoever was aboard this ship. I spotted a rich-looking carriage to the right and noted it must have been sent from the palace. Given the amount of guards loitering around it, that was likely accurate.

Ducking behind a stack of crates, I waited for Grendy to appear in the distance. I didn't need to wait long as she walked down to the dock, in what appeared to be a rapid conversation with Alion. I'd never seen Grendy so animated, and I thought for certain I saw her grab his arm as he scanned the crowd. Was he looking for me? Was she trying to use our cover story on him right now?

Once she reached the bottom of the walkway, the guards stepped forward and surrounded her and Alion. I couldn't tell what was being said, and I could barely see them through the ring, but I suspected that some of the guards knew Alion. That didn't surprise me, as he did seem to be popular wherever he went.

Watching Grendy make her way to the carriage confirmed that our plan was successfully underway. It was time for me to get myself to the farm, where I'd begin the next chapter of my life in this new land.

I turned to slip through the crowd in the opposite direction that the carriage moved in. I had to make sure I took a longer route so as not to be recognized. I may be dressed in sailor garb, but my gait would not pass as one if I stayed around here for too long.

With a jump into an alleyway and a quick change, I pulled my familiar clothing on. I was still wearing Grendy's clothing, yet I didn't mind. I loved the simplicity, and with being on my own in the days to come, it made more sense to wear her clothing, instead of the rich dresses I used to wear.

So, with my travel pack in hand and excitement in my steps, I walked the long, winding road to the place I would begin my new life. It was different, it was nerve-wracking, and it was unreal.

It was time to tend to geese and become the goose girl.

Chapter Ten

Alion

There was someone missing as I stood on the docks with the princess. As the one who needed to escort her down, I almost felt as though her newly animated conversation was a cover. She never expressed this much exuberance before. Perhaps her nerves were in shambles? I couldn't blame her. Surely, meeting a king she was set to marry was enough to bring about this waterfall of words.

She had a firm grip on my arm as she spoke, but I couldn't stop my eyes from scanning the area. Where was her maid? I doubt she had slipped off ahead of us, because I would have spotted her. At least, I'd like to think I would have.

I couldn't deny the connection I had felt with Grendy. She was sassy and abrupt with me, but there were moments I felt such kindness from her. Especially when I saw how she tended to the princess.

"I don't mean to interrupt you, Princess Catalina, but I wondered if you might tell me where your maid has wandered off to?"

The princess froze as we stood on the docks, waiting for the escort to arrive from across the way. Her eyes were unreadable as a mask slid over her face. The smile that appeared seemed like a trained response, and she shone it in my direction.

"Grendy expressed a desire to board the first ship returning to her home. Of course, I hated to see her go, but in my love for her, I thought I should grant her request." Her voice caught for a moment before she continued, "She will be missed, but I'm sure the king will grant me a new maid who shall be up to the task of tending to me in my new role."

Grendy was... gone? Without a word to me, she had just disappeared. It wasn't as though we had a special connection or had ever referred to ourselves as friends, but we had spent a significant amount of time together during our travels.

"Oh, I wasn't aware of that. She seemed so content and well-adjusted to adventure."

Princess Catalina avoided my gaze as she noted a group walking toward us. "You mustn't worry about her. She's so independent and has a very good head on her shoulders. Her training at the palace has done her credit, and she's served me well. I suppose spending time on the ship awakened a sense of adventure in her that she hadn't realized."

"A sense of adventure?" I asked, puzzled. "I thought you said she wanted to go home? Wouldn't that mean she doesn't crave adventure?"

The princess let loose a strained laugh. "Goodness, you analyze words. I just prattle on, so don't pay mine any mind. She said she was homesick, but I sensed she didn't want to leave ship life." She waved her hands as she spoke. "It isn't something I could ever understand, for I've never felt better about having my two legs on solid land. A ship is a horrible business."

An alarm went off in my head, but I was worried I'd rouse suspicion in Catalina if I kept inquiring. After all, to her I was just a ship hand who loved the sea and would likely disappear in a moment as she'd be swept away to see the king she'd soon wed.

I opened my mouth to see if I could inquire about Grendy's whereabouts in a more hidden way. It wasn't as though she was anything special to me; I merely wanted to wish her the best of luck on her travels. Surely, no one could fault me for that. And there was an amount of curiosity in me that needed to be sated.

"Are those the king's guards?" Catalina spoke up, her eyes taking on a special glow as she gestured to the armed men moving closer.

I was running out of time before the news would get out. Even now, a few of them nodded at me as the distance closed. But no matter what I thought of to say, the words wouldn't come out quite right. The guards reached us and I gave a quick shake of my head. Some were already greeting me, but once my expression was noted, the merriment slowed to a halt. It was clear to them that my work had not yet concluded.

Princess Catalina gazed about in awe while some took the luggage that had just been offloaded. Something caught me off guard as I looked around her stack of luggage.

There was not a single piece missing.

My eyes narrowed as I cast a glance at the princess. Something wasn't right here. If Grendy had left, why were there no missing pieces among this pile? I shouldn't know the number they traveled with, but I had been present when they were initially loaded onto the ship. And given my keen eye for numbers and detail, I knew when something wasn't right.

The princess was hiding something. I didn't know why, but somehow, Grendy had left without an item to her name. What had caused that? A quarrel among staff? A miscommunication?

"Your Majesty!" an exuberant voice broke out.

I saw Catalina reel back in surprise. "Most address me as simply princess, so that will do for here as well."

There was silence for a moment before she realized the young guard had been looking in a different direction.

I turned to the princess and gave a smile before offering a slight nod. Taking her hand, I pressed a gentle kiss upon it. "Princess Catalina, may I welcome you to my kingdom, the land of Whyst?"

Part Two

She traded her crown

For but a moment

She saw the king

As an opponent

Yet what she will learn

And what she will feel

Will cause a ripple

She cannot conceal

For now she'll pay

A price so high

To hide this secret

She'll try to deny

Chapter Eleven

Catalina

I walked down the winding road Grendy had instructed me to. It was strange to be alone, as it was not something I generally experienced in my day-to-day life. There was always someone walking with me, watching me, tracking my whereabouts.

For once, there was no one. It was me, alone with the open sky and the surrounding fields. I could already see geese in the distance, flapping their wings and foraging through a patch of wildflowers. I wasn't sure how I felt about geese, but I'm sure any reservations could be pushed aside for the sake of an extended vacation from being engaged to a king.

A king who, as Grendy said, could be terrible. I shuddered at the thought of what the maid had walked into. Princess Catalina had no choice but to follow her royal duty to this land. Goose Girl Lia had the choice of living freely for some time in the countryside. Such sweet relief flooded through me as I considered that.

One thing that did make me happy was the ability to reclaim my own name. Or at least, a version of it. No more being referred to as Grendy. I could be myself again. I could be Lia. Simple, short, and sweet.

With a spring in my step and a whistle on my lips, and in the most unladylike fashion, I quickened my gait until I reached the farm. Raising my hand to knock, I hesitated for a moment. Everything hit me all at once.

How did I know this was safer than staying with a king in a castle? How had Grendy even found out about this farm? What made this a good option for me? The fear brought on so many questions, I could scarcely breathe.

Before I could turn and run, the door flew open, and I was face to face with a strange man. His gray hair was unkempt and would benefit from a brush, and he had a scraggly beard that hung from his face. The tunic he wore had been patched numerous times in more places than I could count, and the smell permeating from it told me it desperately needed a wash.

Or rather, to be thrown straight out.

He looked me over with his own curiosity and I felt awkward under his sharp, alert gaze. How old was this ancient farmer?

"Hello..." I began hesitantly, "I'm Lia."

A smile broke out on his face and his eyes took on a sparkle. "You must be the new goose girl I was told was coming. And right on time too, as my foolish sister seems to have disappeared once more to welcome you. Always traveling the realms with not a care in the world or a thought about her poor, elderly brother."

The words could sound unkind, and they would have if they were spoken by anyone else, but the softness in his voice made them out to be more so the observations of a caring older brother. Observations my own brother would likely make of me. I pushed aside the pang I felt at missing him and tried to direct my full attention to the gentleman in front of me.

"Come now, young lady, I don't bite." He opened the door wider and gestured for me to follow him. "Let's show you to your room and settle you in. You won't start until tomorrow, so just relax while you can."

He was straight to business, and it relieved me. I wouldn't have to think through or engage in small talk—I wouldn't know what to say, anyway. I followed him into the small farmhouse and looked around. It was larger inside than I thought it would be.

It was cluttered, yet somehow clean. Dishes were in a neat stack on the only shelf in the kitchen, and crates of food were next to the small stove in the corner. Yes, this was a man accustomed to living alone, but judging by the frilly curtains and the needlework on the walls, that hadn't always been the case.

"Pardon me, sir." He chuckled at my use of the word sir, but allowed me to go on with no further interruption. "Might you tell me your name?"

"Ah, where are my manners?" He turned and made a bow, as though addressing royalty—which he unknowingly was doing. "My name is Alec. I've been running this farm since I took over from my father—a family business for generations. One my sons will take it over when I pass," he gave a quick wink, "decades from now, of course."

Oh, I was sure to like living here.

He put on a kettle for tea and leaned over to take my bag. "Your room isn't big, but I hope it will do." It was down a short hallway, and he was correct in his description, but the warm quilt on the bed, the soft rug on the floor, and the pretty pictures of embroidered geese on the walls were fitting.

"Now," he turned to me, "I'll leave you to unpack. You may join me for tea after if you wish, or you could take a lie down. Meals are observed promptly on time, but I leave biscuits covered on the counter for a snack if needed. Wash up your own dishes, laundry day is mid-week, and I get food delivered from the market in town, so let me know if you'd like anything specific ordered."

He gave a slight nod, another quick grin, and disappeared, closing the door behind him.

A smile lit my face as I continued to take in the room around me. It was a far cry from my usual style, but there was something so completely familiar about it. As though every piece, every item, had been brought in with such tenderness and love.

I hoisted my bag onto the bed and opened it. Today was for settling in and exploring. Tomorrow, my work as the goose girl would begin.

Chapter Twelve

Catalina

"Come on, you just need to waddle your way over there."

My first day as the goose girl was not progressing as I'd hoped. I'd been pecked twice, released most disgustingly onto three times, and I was sure the gaggle of geese in the corner of the field were gossiping about me right now.

"Would you three cut it out!" I shouted at them.

Their honking stopped, and they looked at me with what I could only interpret as judgmental eyes. One left the gaggle and joined a different group, presumably to gossip some more. At least I could take pride in knowing I had succeeded in separating them.

I stopped suddenly and groaned. I'd been in the field for one day, and already, I was paranoid that these geese were against me. Surely, I was going crazy. That was the only explanation.

I walked down the stretch of the bigger field before reaching where the majority of the geese had gathered. They were chattering as they ducked their heads, foraging and grazing.

My only job here was to make sure that none left the gaggle and all remained safe. That seemed easy enough in theory, but there were two that enjoyed running off on their own adventures. I'd chased them numerous times, and it was only noon.

With that thought, I glanced up. The sun had reached its height in the ocean-blue sky, and my stomach growled in response. I made my way over to a tree and sat down.

When I opened the bag I had packed, there was more than what I had placed in it that morning. My original choice had been three biscuits I had grabbed in a hurry before filling a canteen with water. But what greeted me was a ham and cheese sandwich, a red apple, and the smell of sweet, cold peach tea.

It wasn't a palace meal, and I wasn't sure when Alec had snuck those in, but I sure was grateful. I'd lived in his cottage for a day, and he'd made me feel more welcome than I ever thought possible. And that made this the most delicious meal I had ever enjoyed.

As I sunk my teeth into the first bite, I let my imagination run away with me as I watched the geese. I couldn't help but wonder how Grendy was doing behind the palace walls I saw in the distance.

Not only that, but I wondered how King Falco was doing with the woman he thought was his new bride.

Chapter Thirteen

Falco

P rincess Catalina was filled with so many questions, I could hardly get around to answering them. Gone was the quiet woman aboard the ship we had just disembarked from, replaced by someone so wholly overwhelming, I couldn't think in between her questions.

She made me miss the maid Grendy, with her sharp wit, her quiet, thoughtful expressions, and ready laugh. But I wasn't marrying the maid; I was marrying the princess. It didn't matter how well I felt the maid would suit me, because it was the princess I was with.

"How far is the palace from the harbour?" she asked, interrupting my thoughts.

My assistant must have noticed my blank stare, as he jumped in to answer for me. "The palace is located within twenty minutes of the harbour, fifteen minutes from town, and ten minutes from the local farmland." He then launched into descriptions of each area, and what we were best known for.

I was sure the queen of Maryn had briefed the princess, but she looked to be in rapt attention, as though she'd never heard these facts before. She may be prepared to rule, but they certainly didn't prepare her with much knowledge of the kingdom she would marry into.

In that instant, I felt for her. I couldn't imagine leaving my kingdom to marry a stranger. And yet, her family had shipped her off with scarcely another thought.

Although I should give them more credit than that. In my correspondence with the king of Maryn, I sensed a genuine love for his sister. It seemed desperation had given them little choice as their resources were depleted and their rivers dried.

"You seem so lost in thought, King Falco," Catalina observed sweetly. "Have I upset you?"

"No!" I said abruptly. "Not at all. I'm merely tired from the trip. Going from kingly duties to being a ship hand can be quite a change." I gave her one of my most charming smiles to ease the awkwardness of my sharp answer.

She smiled and nodded. "There's just one thing I can't figure out..."

I'll have to get used to that annoying quality of hers, I thought to myself while waiting for her to continue.

"The men on the ship never hinted at who you were. In fact, they were more than willing to let you get your hands dirty. Why is that?"

I smirked. This was the question I was expecting. It only surprised me that it took her so long to ask. "Yes, well, when you're a fair king willing to pay one's weight in gold, anything is possible."

I expected Catalina to chastise my use of the country's coffers, being from the poor kingdom that she was, but she merely laughed. "I suppose you had your own concerns about the princess you agreed to marry."

"Indeed." I nodded. "I'm glad you see it that way. I couldn't very well marry a stranger." I glanced out the carriage window to see us passing through the farmlands that stretched for miles.

"The way that I am marrying one?"

My eyes snapped back to meet hers, and I was shocked to find them narrowed. The smirk vanished from my face as I grasped this sudden change. I wasn't expecting to see what I saw in her eyes, but there was a hard quality I hadn't noticed before, as though she were sizing me up. I felt uncomfortable.

"I'm sure you understand my position, princess," I commented with a lift in my brow.

"Certainly. A rich king marrying a lowly princess... One cannot be too careful, Your Majesty."

"No," I cut in abruptly. "That is not the way I view it at all." My assistant attempted to make himself look busy by staring out the window, appearing very interested in the colour of the sky.

"Then why not arrange a meeting? If you had so many concerns that you had to stowaway as a mate on a ship, then why not just arrange a meeting with this princess you were so desperate to meet? As it stands, you don't even know if I'm the princess. And how could you know?"

This woman was infuriating, and we'd only truly been together for ten minutes. My next words were slow, as I had to tread carefully. This was my future bride, after all. I was sure the princess had understood my position when we signed the contract. Her role as queen in exchange for my riches.

In fact, I had a letter declaring her loyalty and her acknowledgement that, while she did not bring as much to our union, she would strive to be a queen deserving of my wealth and the life I could afford her. She would want for nothing. And as I looked at the woman before me, I couldn't see the same woman who wrote the letter. Gone was the understanding of our roles in this arrangement.

"Look," I pressed as gently as I could, "we both know what we offer here. I wanted a queen who had no direct claim to the throne since I have all the alliances I need with the neighbouring kingdoms. You wanted wealth and a strong ally. Well, here I am."

She moved to cut in, but I held up one hand. "I know you risked a lot by marrying me. You don't know me, and for all you know, I could have been a cruel and ugly man by nature. You did not have the option of meeting me before, and for that, I am sorry, but should I have foregone the option that my wealth afforded me? Am I to ignore the privilege I have in my life? That hardly seems a fair thing to do, just to accommodate what you are lacking."

Catalina pondered my words carefully before giving a slow nod. "I suppose that's a good enough point. Those who are wealthy take advantage of their privilege, buying their way through life. I cannot begrudge you of that. Please accept my apologies for my temper. I will do better by you in the future." She gave a bow of her head.

The words themselves held an apology, but the tone in her voice did not. If anything, we would get along much less. Somehow, despite us both being royalty, there was a divide here—a lack of understanding about our duty to our crowns. I had hoped there would be a shift in her once she realized it was only desperation that made me stowaway on a ship like that, but as much as I searched her face, there was not.

The chatter I had experienced from her in the beginning of our ride felt like a front she had used to lure me in, only to then show her true opinion of me once I'd been caught. It didn't feel fair.

Thankfully, we were entering the gate to the main courtyard, so there would be no awkward conversation needed to fill in any of our drive. Now she could be shown her chamber to freshen up, and I could take my leave. There was much to be done after my absence, and I may as well start immediately.

Besides... there was a wedding to be had.

Chapter Fourteen

Catalina

It was the end of my second day of work on the farm and I was walking out in the fields, guided by the light of the moon.

In our rush to execute our new plan, we had never actually discussed meeting up with one another. How we would, where we would, when we would. So I decided to wander the fields when darkness set so I could catch her if she happened to show up.

Thankfully, I looked over across the field and saw Grendy making her way over to me. I was relieved that we had both thought of the same thing without needing to say a word. We were like that, though, often in tune with one another.

"Well?" I demanded before she had even stopped before me. "Were we right to trade places?"

She grimaced and gave a slight nod. "It isn't as though he's a monster, princess... but he isn't of the best sort. He uses his riches without a thought and clearly thinks too highly of himself."

"That doesn't sound too terrible. Both qualities that can be reworked, I'm sure."

"Princess," Grendy began before hesitating, "you can't expect to change a man. You have to love someone as they are. Sometimes people change, sometimes they don't. You may find yourself disappointed if you expect him to be a changed man one day."

She had a good point. I started to pace the grass, wondering what step to take next. Obviously, I wanted to remain here for some time. Two days simply wasn't enough time for Grendy to gather the information I needed. I wanted to know more.

"Have you learned how his servants behave around him? I know they will not say much around you, given what they think your status is, but you may have heard things, I'm sure?"

Grendy nodded. "So far, I've heard no complaints. All speak well of him, and he seems to shower much generosity onto his subjects. There are few complaints." She stopped for a moment. "He has an assistant he appears to be very close to, one who often speaks for him."

My brows furrowed and I raised a hand to meet them. I didn't care for a man who let another speak for him, but his generosity did slightly raise my opinion. It wouldn't do to hoard wealth, and if he shared with his subjects willingly, that was something I could focus on in my desire to see his positive qualities.

Really, I had to take what I could get.

"What about his interests?" There were so many questions I had, and while this was probably the least important one, I couldn't hold it in.

"I'm not sure what they are. Truthfully, we haven't spent much time together. He keeps to himself and avoids me."

I reeled back in surprise. "What? But why?"

I saw her eyes shift for a moment, but she merely shrugged. "I don't know. Perhaps it was not his idea to wed—that would explain his absence. But don't worry, it has only been a few days and there is time yet."

"Still," I noted, "it doesn't sit well that during his bride's first days in his land, he doesn't even take the time to help her settle in."

Grendy reached into a pouch I only just noticed her carrying and pulled out a couple of pastries. She sat on the grass and offered me one. She knew if I was pacing, it was time to settle in for a long talk. Or rather, a long period of listening.

"I agree with you, princess, but remember, we all have our own emotions about this experience. And I am not truly his bride."

"But Grendy, don't you see?" I was becoming frustrated. "He doesn't *know* that. For all he knows, you are his bride, and you are here to marry him. It is his duty to create a smooth transition, and he is already failing at the task."

She didn't say much in response, as we both knew I was right. I took a vindicated bite of the pastry, only realizing then that I had no idea what I was biting into. How fitting for our current situation. I was relieved to be met with a familiar taste and enjoyed the delightful strawberry and rhubarb flavour that melted in my mouth.

"I understand what you're saying and your words hold truth, to be sure. You will not hear further argument from me. He should be present and he should be engaging, but he is not."

I continued my pacing as I watched her pull out yet another treat from the bag, followed by a canteen and two mugs. Had she planned an entire picnic for us?

At my one raised brow, she offered a smile. "I didn't know what kind of fare you enjoyed the last few days. A maid's work is never done, even when that maid is a princess."

It was nice to share a laugh with Grendy after the strange weeks we'd had together. If those back home knew how far we had taken this ruse, we would be in endless trouble. Perhaps we would even be forced to separate. But it was a secret we would keep until it was safe to reveal, and I felt immense relief at that.

"Come, princess, let us take a break from the questions. I've brought some of your favourites, and a midnight picnic is not something we've ever enjoyed together before."

She was right. Here, in the middle of a new land, with the moon directly above us and stars twinkling their stories, we could enjoy yet another new experience with each other.

How sweet it was to have a best friend, who cared so deeply for me, that she would not only trade places to protect me, but keep introducing me to delightful new experiences.

I raised my mug of cider. "To the maid who is always dedicated to my well-being."

She raised hers in response. "And to the princess who has always treated me as the dearest of friends."

"In body and in soul," we finished together, our Maryn toast following us to the fields of Whyst.

Chapter Fifteen

Falco

Perhaps it didn't make me groom of the year, but I avoided my intended bride after our official meeting. The awkward conversation in the carriage bothered me to no end, and while I would have liked to put it behind us, I had no idea how to go about that. She was entirely different from her letter had portrayed. I knew I couldn't base a person off one letter, but I was so convinced that I'd accurately learned her character through it.

Another lesson learned, I suppose.

I suppose I should blame myself, seeing as how I could have spent more time with her aboard the ship. She was just so awkward during that time. I thought it was to do with moving to a new land or being on a ship at sea for the first time, but truthfully, she was just awkward. I felt uncomfortable.

Was I now to spend my life with a woman I had nothing in common with and never felt at ease with? Was this how I was to be thanked for saving another kingdom with my riches?

With a groan, I lifted my head to the clock above the fireplace. The sun was setting, and I knew that meant I'd need to prepare for dinner. It was a private dinner with just Catalina and I—something I had arranged before I even left the castle in order to get to know one another. Two weeks of private dinners leading up to the wedding, followed by a honeymoon in my mountain palace, which was a two-day journey from here.

The last three dinners had passed in silence. The arrival dinner had been quiet and icy. Her clear disdain for me was shocking. She resented my riches, yet her country benefited from them—and the irony was not lost on me. I tried to engage her many times, but it was of no use.

The second dinner I inquired if she'd explored the grounds. She said the head housekeeper had given her a tour, and it was very well kept. I asked if anything particular had caught her interest, and her flat response in the negative killed off any further conversation.

The third night was interesting. She rushed through the meal, acting as though she had some place to be. Her normally pale face was flushed, and her eyes darted around as though tracking the time.

I wondered to myself if she was meeting someone? Who could she possibly have become friends with in such a short amount of time? My valet had told me she'd mostly kept to her rooms, outside of the tour the morning after our arrival.

I asked her if all was well and she gave a quick nod, words rushing from her after. "Yes, yes. Quite well. Just find myself quite liking this—" She paused and looked down, startling herself. "Liver and..." she peered closer, "fish eggs?" she finished lamely, her disgust clear on her face.

Now I knew something peculiar was going on. No one was eager to finish such a meal. The only reason the cook continued to prepare it as an appetizer was due to the fact that it was a tradition of our nation. One that began in our earliest years as a kingdom, when we were dirt poor and had nothing in our coffers.

No one actually ate the appetizer; it was our form of saying a blessing over the table. We took a bite of each, drank the country's richest cider, and signaled the end of the course. From the richest home to the poorest farm, this was our custom. It was the reason I sent a weekly delivery of liver, fish eggs, and cider to the less wealthy districts.

Catalina clearly did not know this fact, which proved to be even more suspicious to me. Especially considering the very topic had been mentioned in her letter to me. Something wasn't right here.

As soon as the dinner had ended, she'd stood suddenly, curtsied, and said, "Thank you for the lovely meal," before she rushed away. I moved to follow at a distance, but my steward arrived to deliver a letter. With a hurried glance down, I saw it was addressed to me by the king of Maryn.

Catalina's brother was likely inquiring if she had arrived safely. Surely, he'd heard from his own men, but he wanted communication to remain open, so with one last glance at Catalina's retreating form, I began my walk to the study.

A knock on the door pulled me from my thoughts of the previous dinner. I was still mulling over my response to King Enrich and his strange request.

He was offering some resources to construct a stained-glass hall as a wedding gift to Catalina. It seemed a strange gift, but apparently, it had been her favourite room in her former home. When the sunlight shone through, rainbows danced across the walls, lighting everything with an ethereal glow... or so the king claimed.

I supposed it was something I could bring up to Catalina. Not to spoil the surprise, merely to claim I'd heard of this grand hall. If it was something that would help our union—if she knew how eager I was to maintain a civil relationship—then perhaps we could find a common ground.

"Sire?" My steward appeared. "You've run out of time to change. She is waiting for you."

I'd completely lost track of time and it likely wouldn't help her opinion of me, especially as I'd been avoiding her during the day. I placed the papers I'd gone through today in a stack and made a note for where to pick up tomorrow.

Dusting off my jacket, I straightened my shoulders and began my walk through the castle to the king and queen's private dining chamber.

She was seated in the queen's chair, staring down at the plate before her, likely realizing it was a plate of liver and fish eggs again.

"Good evening, Princess Catalina."

We moved through the usual pleasantries as I inquired about her day. She did not inquire of mine, but I was used to her silence. She thought I was a rich snob, yet she was the one snubbing me. *How rich.*

"Something I've been meaning to talk about is the stunning stained-glass hall I've heard so much about that resides in the kingdom of Maryn."

There was no outward display of excitement at my words, merely a very unladylike shrug and a comment of, "Alright."

"I hear it is a beautiful display of handiwork created by one of the first kings as a declaration of love to the queen. And now it is a piece of art that many travel to see from far away."

She took a second bite of fish eggs and I saw her revulsion as she chewed, wincing slightly at the texture. "It is beautiful, to be sure, but yet another display of wealth and riches. Funds that surely could have been used elsewhere."

Now I was completely dumbfounded. I turned my attention to the plate before me, taking a bite of the traditional fare before signaling for the next course.

Catalina's comical relief at the removal of the first course did nothing to derail my thought process. She didn't care about any stained-glass hall. She did not seem to care about any mention of her homeland at all.

My eyes narrowed as she took a sip of water from a crystal glass she'd been toying with. There was something very wrong here.

Princess Catalina was fooling someone, and I highly doubted it was her brother.

In fact, I was certain she was fooling me.

Chapter Sixteen

Falco

It took me all of twenty-four hours to make a decision about my next steps. First, I needed to figure out where she was going every night. Then, I needed to decide what I would do about it. Because until I could figure out her destination, I wouldn't know how to go about doing anything. For all I knew, she just liked to wander after a meal. Perhaps, in her land, it was perfectly normal to run off like that in the dark of night. Not safe... but normal.

I took out a piece of paper and addressed the top to King Enrich. I felt much confusion about Catalina's response to the stained-glass hall. Based on what King Enrich had said, she should have been falling over with excitement over the mere mention of it. And yet, she had shrugged as casually as if I had just told her we were expecting rain the following afternoon.

I raised my hand to my forehead and massaged the creases I knew were there from the tension I felt in my current situation.

I hadn't expected this to be easy, but I certainly thought it would fall into place better. I felt a connection to Catalina. Or at least, I had based on what I'd been told about her and my limited interaction through a letter.

The letter was locked away in my quarters, but I smiled at the recollection of it.

I look forward to our union and what it offers to our countries, Your Majesty. I have studied earnestly to give Whyst a queen worth having, and I hope you are pleased by the results of my hard work. Together, we will rule well and provide for our subjects, for I already think of them as ours, not just yours.

Yes, Catalina had seemed like a queen who would offer so much to Whyst. Her willingness to adopt my people as her own without even stepping foot on these lands had warmed my heart. She had confirmed my decision to choose my queen, not based on her wealth, her kingdom, or her beauty, but based on her heart.

When I was presented with the idea of pursuing a union with the kingdom of Maryn, my correspondence with them became important. While most letters had been exchanged with King Enrich, this one special letter was the one that made me fall for her—if such a thing was possible through a letter. One single letter was all it had taken for me to think so fondly of her and look forward to our union.

I stared at King Enrich's name at the top of my page. How could I put into words what I was thinking when I wasn't even sure of the situation? I couldn't very well accuse him of misrepresenting his sister; the insult would be too difficult to recover from and it wouldn't to do paint our union with a brush so early on.

I could discreetly inquire after her nighttime walks; ask if perhaps some sights in Maryn were only appreciated at night. Or I could dig deeper about this stained-glass hall. Perhaps he only imagined his sister's fascination with it. A tale he shared to add some romance to a marriage that we all knew was arranged, despite us making the best of it.

Having my thoughts interrupted by yet another knock at the door was infuriating. I would need to incorporate a do-not-disturb issue if these kept up. I knew there would be interruptions with a wedding coming up, but given the time I intended to take off for my upcoming honeymoon, surely they knew I had plenty of work to do before then.

"Sir, there is someone here to see you."

"You must be mistaken. I have no engagements on my schedule today."

My steward hesitated and awkwardly glanced around the room. "It is not someone who can be put off, Your Majesty."

I raised an eyebrow. Was my future queen already so demanding? But no, if it had been her, she wouldn't need an announcement. She would be welcome to walk in. "Very well, then. Send this person in."

A large man entered the room. He was intimidating at first glance, and his expression showed he was not someone to be crossed. I had never seen this man before in my life, and already, I wanted to offer him my chair as I rose for an introduction.

He barely gave the room a glance as he nodded at me, his face breaking out in an easy grin. It seemed that, despite my assumption of his intimidating nature, one could not help but gravitate to such a charming smile. My eyes narrowed slightly. I didn't need the trouble a charming smile could bring.

The man strode forward until he was standing in front of my desk and uncharacteristically stuck his hand out. He wished to shake the hand of a *king*? This was becoming stranger by the minute. He had bracelets on his arms that shook from the movement as I grasped his hand in my own.

His forward attitude was becoming too much, but if that wasn't worse, he glanced down at the papers on my desk, his eyes catching on the blank page with the name on top. Surprise came across his features as he caught my eyes once more.

"Forgive me, sir," I began pointedly. "Can I help you, or is there something specific you're after? My steward failed to fill me in on your reason for being here."

"Seems like you may have summoned me yourself." He smiled with a twinkle in his eye as he nodded at the letter I had begun.

There was no measuring stick to take in the length of my confusion as I looked him over. Simple travel clothing, elaborate jewelry, and rich brown hair. I knew no one who fit such a strange description.

"I'm afraid I don't understand your meaning..."

He gave a tilt of his head before offering yet another charming smile. "I am King Enrich. And my sister will not be expecting my visit."

Chapter Seventeen

Falco

I f I'd been holding a beverage, it would have crashed down in that moment. The king of Maryn was here, in my office. I'd received no notice of a visit, no indication that he had intended to make this trip, and showing up unannounced showed signs of distrust, in my opinion. Catalina had mentioned nothing at all.

Although he had just stated she wouldn't be expecting him...

"What is the meaning of this?" I demanded, gesturing for him to take a seat. I wasn't sure how to address him, as calling him king seemed too formal for an almost brother-in-law, yet calling him by his given name was most certainly too friendly.

He sat down, still eyeing the letter I'd begun, a more serious expression on his face. "I decided to come for the wedding. As a surprise."

"A surprise?" I questioned. "It's a month-long journey. You had to have left shortly after your sister. And you do realize how difficult it is to keep a visit from royalty as a surprise. Surely, your sister knew you were here as soon as you stepped foot inside this palace."

"Perhaps," he conceded. "I would not put it past her to already have half the staff in love with her and ready to do her bidding." He ignored my statement about his departure from Maryn.

I started at his words. That didn't sound like Catalina at all. "Forgive me, but how would she manage that when she scarcely leaves her rooms?"

Enrich's brows furrowed as he looked over at me, his eyes finally leaving the empty letter. "You must be mistaken. I'm sure you've just missed it, given how much time is spent in a king's office."

His implication at my not paying enough attention to my intended stung a bit. I was doing my best, but Catalina had not made it easy to form any kind of connection since her arrival. I was doing everything I could during our dinners together, but it wasn't enough.

"I take dinner with my bride every evening, King Enrich." The formal name it was to be. "She is not particularly warm, but I can understand her hesitation and desire to hide away, given she is in a new land."

He picked up a paperweight that had been placed on top of a stack of unsigned documents, waiting for my attention. "That's odd. She shed many tears on her farewell, but she reportedly expressed excitement at exploring her new home."

Finally, an answer to her nighttime wanderings, then. She was shy and wanted to explore without anyone nearby. It did make some sense.

"What could you be thinking with that expression, King Falco?" It was asked in a friendly manner, but with an edge that no one would dare not answer.

"Just that it explained her late-night walks..."

Enrich laughed, and when he realized I was serious, it died away as quickly as it had begun. "You're not serious. Lina spends her evenings with her nose in a book. She would never willingly put a book down and leave the confines of the castle. Not to mention, it would jeopardize her safety."

Now I had even more questions. Catalina had not appeared to have read a single book in her lifetime. When I'd inquired of her reading the night before, her nose had wrinkled in distaste. There was not a single conversation that could be had with her. Everything was a dead end.

"How long have these walks been going on for?" He frowned. "And where does she go?"

My day had begun at odds with my bride and ended with her brother sitting at my desk, asking the very question I'd wondered myself. This whole arrangement was arousing suspicion. Something wasn't right here, not with Catalina and not with her brother showing up—and not just a brother, but a king with his own kingdom to run.

"The first night she retired to her rooms quite early. However, since the second night, she has gone on walks. Yesterday was our fourth night together, and she left then, too. I was not able to follow her as I only just received your letter about the stained-glass hall."

Finally, a satisfied smile lit Enrich's face. "Ah, perfection. I'm sure that brought about much laughter and excitement."

It was as though this man didn't know his own sister. Laughter and excitement? From Catalina? It was as I suspected... One of us didn't know her true self, and I was sure it was me. The question was, why?

"There were comments on the misuse of finances with the construction of such an elaborate display..."

The king's expression froze. "That makes no sense. Catalina knows we only put forth what we can afford, and the resources come from our own making. The funds would be yours, but the materials our own. It is this very labour that provides work for our people. She would know this."

Silence fell over us both as we considered what was going on. I'm sure neither of us intended to regard the other with such blatant suspicion, but it was hard not to.

"Something is very wrong here," he finally commented.

I could only grunt my agreement at his very obvious statement. What was there to say when there was even more to think about than when he had stepped foot in this room.

"We must follow her tonight," I stated in the end. "I will dine with her, and you will join me once she leaves."

He nodded. "I would like to give my sister her privacy as she deals with her adjustment, but I cannot ignore what you've shared. It alarms me."

"Remain in this study; I will instruct no one to speak of your presence. At any rate, if she hasn't heard of your arrival, we can at least stall for the few hours it will take to get to the bottom of this."

He laughed sarcastically. "A few hours? My, you are confident."

"Yes, it's one of my winning qualities." I offered a slight bow and walked around my desk. "She will be expecting me soon, and I must ready myself for our meal. I'll have my steward bring you something."

"Thank you, King Falco."

"Please," I added, "it is just Falco for family. If that is what we are to become at the end of this mystery, then please address me as such."

"Very well. I expect the same from you."

We parted ways under a spell of confusion as we both pondered what was happening. Neither of us shared many thoughts, and there was a general awkwardness surrounding the situation. I could only hope we would resolve this tonight.

Chapter Eighteen

Falco

"Enrich," my voice came out in a low whisper, "have you joined me yet?" The room was dark as I knew Catalina would never leave if she saw lights on in my main rooms.

"I am here."

We didn't say much else, just slowly made our way down the hall until we were around the corner from the door she would soon exit. I raised a finger to my lips and he nodded, and we turned to watch and wait. A few maids rushed past, casting us strange looks, and I merely gave them a quick smile before they continued on their way. I'm sure they were used to my strange antics by now.

Nearly an hour passed, and I had nearly given up my desire to wait when, suddenly, her door swung open. She wore a hood that shrouded her face, and her form turned up and then down the hall, likely looking to catch sight of anyone who may be about. Thankfully, we were hidden in the shadows, and she began her walk toward the back of the castle, just as I suspected she would.

I gestured for Enrich to follow as we slowly crept between every open doorway we could. We didn't make a sound, and I had the royal hunting parties to thank for that. I wasn't sure what Enrich's skills were, but it almost frightened me at how silent he was, and it took everything in me not to constantly glance over my shoulder to make sure he was still behind me.

We followed Catalina down endless passages and through the kitchen, where she filled a bag with some food. *How odd.* Then she walked out a side door I'd never been through before. It was strange to think she knew about an exit I did not. What else had she discovered after being here scarcely a week?

We paused before opening the door she disappeared through, unsure if she would hesitate on the other side. Finally, after counting to ten, I risked opening it as slowly as possible, looking through the crack, just in time to watch her disappear over the servant's bridge.

With a rush, we hurried after her. It was much easier to follow her out here with only the moon as a guide and more elements to hide behind to avoid being spotted.

Enrich quickly dove into a shrub, pulling me along by my sleeve just as Catalina turned to look over her shoulder. His reflexes and intuition made me even more curious about his skill set on a hunt, but there wasn't a moment to think, because just as quickly as he pulled me into hiding, he was pulling me out to keep moving.

"This is most strange," Enrich whispered when we finally made it to where Catalina was traveling to. She had stopped in a field and was standing, as though waiting for someone.

"Is she perhaps meeting someone of interest? Was there another she loved before she came?" As much as I had disliked my time with her, it did pain me to consider she may not have come as willingly as what had been communicated to me.

"There was no one. Catalina's interests lie purely in books, art, music, and such... as well as any new endeavor her mind can take up. She is a woman of a constantly changing mind."

"Is it possible you missed something?"

He bristled at the question and looked at me as though I'd sprouted a second head. "I know you have no family to speak of, Falco, and I am sorry for that, but we are a close family. There is nothing we keep from one another."

"Forgive me." I bowed slightly. "But your statement appears to have holes in it, given we are currently pursuing your sister in the dead of night for reasons you do not know." I wouldn't deny his claim to my lack of family; I had ascended to my throne at the age of sixteen after a regency that was twelve years old—that was how long I had been without my family. At twenty-three, I couldn't remember what it was like to have that feeling. Hence why marriage had appealed to me at so young an age. That, and needing an heir.

"Perhaps her stay here has caused her some troubles," he pointed out, interrupting my stream of thoughts.

I wouldn't argue with him on that matter, as it was obvious she was showing both of us two very different people. The princess Enrich spoke of seemed warm, friendly, knowledgeable, and, dare I say, somewhat flighty with her interests. Yet, the one I knew had no interests and was about as warm as a marble floor in the middle of winter.

"Wait." I held up my hand before Enrich could continue his chatter on the importance of his family matters. "Someone appears to be coming. So she is meeting someone here who—"

"No," he gasped suddenly.

"Do you know them?"

"That walk is so familiar," he muttered to himself, "but it can't be because..."

With both figures hooded, this suspense was killing me as we lay ducked behind a hill, while I tried to ignore the remnants that remained from the geese that must occupy it during the day.

After what felt like ages, both figures removed their hoods, and I was shocked at who I saw. "*Grendy*?" The maid from the ship who I had developed such delightful banter with? Who I couldn't stop comparing Catalina to? "She's come to meet Grendy?"

Enrich's head turned in my direction so quickly, I was scared he would snap it himself from the reflex. "Surely, this cannot be."

"What? You don't think a maid would rather work in a goose field as her princess moves to an even grander castle?" I questioned sarcastically. Perhaps we weren't as suited for one another as I'd imagined. The grass was always greener on the other side. If she really was someone who craved a simpler life, it was a good thing destiny had sought to separate us.

Suddenly, Catalina called out to the one who had just removed her hood. "Catalina, thank goodness. You're late."

Wait... The world began to move in slow motion as I looked between the two figures and then to Enrich. His expression was speculative, as though wondering if I had always been such a slow thinker.

The one I had called Grendy had a quick retort. "Well, it isn't as though you've been working in a field all day, Grendy. Some of us are used to finer things in life still." Laughter echoed up to us, and I froze in place as this new information washed over me.

"You have not been dining with the princess, Falco," Enrich pointed out, as though I was too stupid to realize that for myself.

"She's not the princess," I finally whispered. Catalina was Grendy; Grendy was Catalina. They had traded places. But why? What was so terrible about marrying me that had Catalina running for the hills, literally, as she tended geese all day? I pulled my thoughts together and whipped my head to face Enrich, anger showing on my features.

"You'd best tell me what is going on and why you're really here, Enrich. And no more silly tales of family togetherness."

Chapter Nineteen

Falco

Enrich gestured for me to follow him farther away from where the princess and the maid were conversing. "Not too close to them. We must speak plainly, and it would be best if we returned to the lodgings."

"I will retreat a few more paces, but I will not leave until I have the full story." My voice raised slightly, and he quickly raised his hands to placate me. "What do you think is stopping me from running down there immediately and questioning both of them? Questioning all of you!"

"Please, Falco, Catalina has no knowledge of my being here, nor why I am truly here."

"So you admit it isn't about a stained-glass hall."

He hesitated and I took a step toward the field. "No, no," he rushed out, "I do intend to offer resources to construct such a hall. My sister deserves a piece of her homeland, since she has done so much for our kingdom in this marriage."

"We will see if such a marriage will take place…"

"Let's not be hasty. I am prepared to share the full story, but it's awkward to begin and, as yet, it has no end. Only my arrival here to ascertain my sister's safety, which I have now done."

"Safety? You want to speak of safety?" I couldn't keep the bewilderment from showing on my face. "Your sister is living in an old man's hut—if my assumption is correct that these are indeed the fields of Alec's family goose business—and has spent her last days herding geese. Not to mention, her time aboard the ship. Learning how to sail, cook, mend, and so on. Safety would be surrounding her with guards—"

"She is safe here."

"I will fetch her this instant."

Enrich's hand reached out and grasped my arm. "We cannot."

"So we are to leave the princess… no, the future queen of Whyst, in a field filled with goose droppings?"

Enrich looked over the hill we'd been resting behind, taking in our surroundings and the grounds we stood on, which stretched on for miles. "I see lush fields, a nice pond, and no droppings in sight." His demeanor was almost too pleasant. Almost as though he felt relieved.

"How can you take this so calmly? A moment ago you were as shocked as I was."

Enrich sighed and then nodded in my direction, without meeting my gaze. "About a year ago, there were whisperings of an uprising. Not from our people, but those who are a part of

Zenyth. They have been forming as a democracy in response to their people's protests against the monarchy. In those dealings, they have decided to do away with all monarchs, even those in neighbouring lands."

"I know of such things. They have approached us in the past, although not for long, given the size of my armies and the ships in my harbour."

"They made us an offer or threatened to cut off the main river that flows through their kingdom and into ours," Enrich continued. "This river offers most of our fertile growing lands the nourishment it needs through our hottest seasons. It flows from their tallest mountain range, which sees snowfall every year. We have a mountain that feeds a lake near our castle, but beyond that, we do not see snowfall yearly, and we have now run low since we declined their offer.

"I have done what I can to see us through these times, but there were raids near our border. Farms burned to the ground, families displaced, livelihoods lost. I sought a solution and knew you were looking for a bride, which is why I put forth Catalina as a candidate. They continued their attacks up until the betrothal agreement was signed. Instead, they focused their attention on ridding Maryn and Whyst of Catalina—they sought to end her life. Many attempts were made, all thwarted by myself before she could learn of them. I thought she would be safer here, with you. And now she is in a field pretending to be someone else, and I cannot think of anything safer."

I was shocked at the words he was sharing with me. There was a threat to her life? This was insane. I knew our agreement involved importing goods and filling their treasury, but I assumed that was merely what marriage entailed. I was receiving a strong, educated queen for my country, and they were benefiting from my riches—a good arrangement. I had no idea the desperation that this agreement was made from, saving her life and the kingdom.

"So Catalina made the sacrifice to marry me and avoid such catastrophe for her people, with no knowledge that she herself was in danger? And now, you are here because you suspect that threat on her life is still present?"

He turned to watch Catalina and Grendy in the field as they sat on a blanket, and Catalina, no, Grendy, handed Catalina pastries, buns, and cheese. A canteen was removed, and I immediately knew it was the rich cider Grendy had enjoyed so much with our dinners.

My eyes fixated on Catalina—the real Catalina. This girl, who was a princess from a traditional land, who had traded lives with a common maid of her own and lived the last month as though she had no more responsibility than anyone else.

Part of me was angry. Was the idea of me so appalling to her that she could not imagine a life with me? True, I had stowed away on a ship to get to know my future bride, but a lot of good that had done me, since she had somehow foiled my attempts in the end. Perhaps that was what made me angrier. I thought I had the superior plans, yet here she was, and I was only just realizing it now. Over a month had passed since we left the shores of Maryn, and only now was I learning who she truly was.

However, part of me was empathetic. I understood the desire to live a more simple life, free from responsibility, free from duty. Answering to no one but myself as I followed what I wanted to do and what my own interests were. True, I was a king and I could do as I pleased, but I couldn't go off to study astronomy. I couldn't take up a team sport in the village; I couldn't participate in a baking contest. Those were all things I had wanted to try throughout my days, but I never could.

Being Alion on that ship had afforded me much, like the opportunity to get to know a humble maid who sought to learn the simple lessons life could offer. I had learned how to ready a chicken with her. We had tied knots together. I'd watched her attempt to darn socks. All had gone poorly, but she'd been an eager, ready learner. Perhaps that was a quality I wanted in a queen now.

Enrich broke through my thoughts once more. "I suppose we go back to the castle and attempt to keep my identity hidden until it's safe to extract Catalina. It will be hard to sit and wait, but it might be our best chance."

"Wait..." I spoke up. "I have a better idea."

"Hello, I wondered if you were hiring a goose boy for your fields."

The man looked me up and down as he blinked a few times. I couldn't tell if he recognized me, but hopefully in my farming clothes, all other smoothness could be overlooked. I rushed to fill in the blanks. Thankfully, I knew every farmer in this area, though it had been some time since I'd visited.

"My name is Alion. I know you recently hired on a goose girl, and as I've arrived back from a month-long voyage, I, too, seek employment."

"You look familiar," he cut in with a friendly smile.

"I'm sure you are mistaken." I raised an eyebrow to challenge him, only to be met with another in return.

"Right. Well, whoever you are is no matter to me. I have a goose girl, Lia, working now, and if you wish to join, she could use another. I can't pay as high a wage as hers, but if you don't mind being her second, you're welcome here. Do you have your own lodgings?"

This was proving to be easier than I thought.

Chapter Twenty

Catalina

"You've got to be kidding me!" My loud call of frustration could be heard clear across the field, and I cared so very little for that fact. "I've separated you three numerous times, and I won't tolerate anymore disrespect from you. Honest to goodness, you've got to be—"

My voice cut off as my foot landed in yet another delightful pile I should have avoided. The loud, repetitive squawks I heard provoked me even more. "Did you leave this here on purpose? Why I've half a mind to..." my voice trailed off in Grendy fashion as shouts turned into mumbles.

I was at the end of my first week in this field, and it still shocked me how I could take what these geese did personally. Deep down, I was almost certain they weren't out to get me, but there was something in their strange mannerisms that still made me feel their actions were very intentional.

I leaned down and brushed the fresh droppings from my shoes. The shoes were nothing special, but my other pair was still drying from yesterday's incident, which mirrored today's in much a similar fashion. One could only hope I wouldn't have to remain barefoot for tomorrow.

I heard tittering across the field, and I felt the last of my patience wear through. "I'm telling you, once I'm through here, I'll march right home to Alec and tell him what a delightful stew you'll make!"

A chuckle sounded behind me and I spun in shock, hopping on one foot as droppings fell from the stick I'd been using as a scraper. I didn't realize I wasn't alone and, in my shock, I fell right over into the very same pile I'd promised to cook a goose for.

"Alion?" I gasped in surprise.

"The very same." His smooth voice made my embarrassment even more pronounced as I sat there in shock. His hand reached down to me as he closed the distance, grabbing my hand without even asking if I needed help.

"What on earth are you doing here?"

"Well, that's a delightful welcome for an old friend."

I blushed. "Pardon me, I had no intention of being rude, but you did come out of nowhere. And whether you were welcome or not, you're still not meant to be here."

His hand came to his chest. "Your words wound me. How do you know I haven't just hunted the kingdom to find you?"

I couldn't resist rolling my eyes at Alion's words. Always so friendly, always so charming; there was no denying the attractive nature of this ship hand.

"Wait, aren't you working on the ships still?"

"No, I've found a new occupation."

It was something of a relief to hear because, despite my not knowing much about how ships operated, he really did do his job as a deckhand very poorly.

"Well, you were somewhat of a liability to any ship that took you on." His shocked expression made me laugh, and I rushed into my question. "And what occupation would that be?"

He gestured around us to the fields and the geese that filled them. "I'm to be your new partner to wrangle these geese in." He looked past me to the gaggle that sat behind me. "Particularly those whom you wish to make into a stew."

"Alec hired you on to assist me? He made no such mention this morning."

"Did he not? How odd." It was then that I realized one of his hands still held fast to mine, and I rushed to withdraw it. "Perhaps the surprise is better than knowing?"

I turned away from him in an effort to hide whatever emotions would play across my face. I don't know why I would be so excited at the prospect of spending time with Alion. I hadn't wanted to admit it, even to myself, but after being on the ship with him for a month, my days had felt surprisingly dull once he was absent from them. Of course, there was no sense in acknowledging it.

He'd been so willing to spend time together, to learn everything I was learning in the kitchens. He was the one who made me feel like I was so much more than just Princess Catalina Marionotti. With him, I could gut a chicken, tie sailing knots, fix old furniture, and so much more.

Perhaps there were no deeper feelings than my appreciation that there had been someone who had witnessed all I could do when I wasn't just a princess, when I didn't have to abide by the same limitations day in and day out. When I was free to make something of myself.

"Grendy?"

Alion's voice cut in and I turned back to him, startling out of my own thoughts. I should probably converse with him to keep up this lovely facade. But first things first...

"Actually, my name is Lia." A lie. "Grendy is just a... nickname." Another lie. What could I say? I had to protect my identity somehow, and why would he care? He was a ship hand, likely hailed from a nearby farm where he'd grown up... someone like me. Or rather, someone very much like who I wanted to be.

"Lia," he started with a smile. "You've got droppings on your cheek."

Chapter Twenty-One

Catalina

I couldn't understand Alion's strange moods. One day he was perfectly content to laugh and pass time in these fields, yet at other moments he was moody and temperamental. Our first day was a mix between the familiarity of the ship and the awkwardness of officially working together in the fields.

There wasn't much I could recall from the first day, but as we worked with one another in the following days, it felt as though he was holding back. We would ease into the lighthearted banter we enjoyed on the ship, and then suddenly, he would pull away.

I tried to tell myself it was likely some situation at home that couldn't be helped, but I think deep down, I knew better. Being on that ship felt like an eternity ago, but really, it had only been a week or so.

Today, he confused me yet again when he reached up to brush a stray lock of hair away from my face, a smile lighting his own.

"Do you ever think of wearing your hair back with anything other than a ribbon?"

I laughed, but in truth, there wasn't much I could say to that. How was I supposed to admit that I didn't know how to do my own hair? A princess was taught how to sit, how to walk, how to dictate herself, how to respect foreign customs, but she simply was not taught how to do her own hair.

He shook his head as I avoided answering and looked across the fields. "Those three geese have been oddly quiet today."

"Probably just plotting my murder..." I muttered under my breath.

"What was that?" he asked.

"Uh, nothing. Just saying that I hope the rain stays away..."

His eyes narrowed and he smirked. We both knew that wasn't what I'd said at all.

A gust of wind blew out of nowhere, and the hat he wore to keep his dark hair at bay flew off his head. He scrambled after it, and I raised my voice to sing the tune I always did when this happened, for it happened multiple times by now.

Come winds, come gusts
Steal what you may
Blow the hats all away
Til the night comes
And my hair may lay
Atop my head after today

He turned to me in annoyance as he rushed to catch it. "I'm not entirely convinced it's not you causing this."

"Why, Alion! I'm as innocent as a goose."

"Which goose, is the question..."

"That is the question, indeed." I smirked at him while running my hands through my hair, the ribbon having flown off with the first gust of wind that morning.

This was the way of our days—the few we had spent together, at any rate. He would tease and I would smile; he would pull back and I would question. He would laugh and I would melt; he would turn away and I would wonder.

I should be infuriated, but in truth, I was more curious than anything else. What could be causing this man so much hesitation that he would enjoy his time and then grow silent at a moment's notice? Was it something to do with me, after all?

My initial assumption was that it didn't, but what did I know? All I knew of Alion was that he'd worked on a ship and now he worked in a field. In all our time aboard that ship, we never really dove into who we were. At the time, that suited me fine, given I was pretending to be a maid. Currently, I wasn't pretending as much as I had been then.

I was a goose girl in a field, but I didn't have to pretend to be a maid, and here I could just go by Lia—no fake name and no playing pretend. Just spending my days in a field avoiding the king I would inevitably marry.

There was a part of me that wanted to go on forever living this simple life, but I knew there was no way I could continue this for more than even a week. I was tempting fate by having this go on for so long to begin with.

"Lia? Are you returning to this realm today?"

Somehow I had completely lost focus and, in that time, he'd returned with his hat and was standing closer to me than I recalled experiencing. I startled back and jumped up, needing to place distance between us. He was a nice enough man, but given my impending marriage, there was little point in forming an attachment.

Besides, I reminded myself as I strode farther away from him, *he's not your usual type.*

Although, I was having a more difficult time believing that the more I got to know him.

Chapter Twenty-Two

Falco

F inding Lia in the field the morning I began was nothing
short of delightful. There she was, with her golden hair
tied back, stray locks framing her face. She had feathers stuck
to her, she was screaming obscenities at geese, there were droppings on her, and she had never looked more beautiful.

This was the princess; this was the woman I had chosen to
be the queen of Whyst. A woman with no regard for what was
proper, no care for the finer things in life, and who seemed
perfectly content to spend her days yelling at geese.

How on earth could I have gotten so lucky?

Yet, there was something that held me back every day that I
spent with her. On one hand, I felt bad leaving her maid back
at the castle, posing as my bride. It was true that Enrich felt it
was safer if no one knew, and I'd paid the staff a fine amount of
gold to keep things quiet, but here the maid was, pretending to
be my bride, and I was out chasing geese.

What I couldn't understand was that the real Grendy hadn't figured it out yet. Wouldn't Catalina have told Grendy she was working with Alion from the ship? Grendy would have immediately known it was me and suspected something. She seemed wise enough to figure out what was going on... if she knew.

I couldn't very well ask either of them as that would give me away, but I was left to wonder why Catalina said nothing and why Grendy did not seem to care that I was apparently locked away in my office every day. She made no effort to see me, and I had to admit that I didn't care, either. We just did not care for each other, and it was a fact that relieved me now that I knew the truth.

There was another problem that presented itself, though. A new issue I hadn't seen coming but did make sense, given our current situation. And that was, why was Lia choosing this instead of me?

The more time I spent with her in the fields watching geese, the more I came to resent her. Now that her brother had confirmed exactly who she was, I could no longer handle the mixed emotions this information brought out in me.

She had never even met me, yet she had decided without a second thought that the mere idea of marriage was off the table. As though she thought the concept of me so ugly, so detestable, she could never bind herself to me, despite the riches my kingdom could offer her.

There were no benefits for me when it came to securing an alliance with Maryn; in fact, it was the exact opposite—it took more beneficial matches off the table for me. Instead of finding someone I could wed for more power, more connections, more wealth, I had been willing to tie myself to a lesser kingdom that offered me nothing.

And for what?

For her to switch places with her maid and run off to sit in a field all day watching geese. The alternative was so ghastly to her, she would rather do this every single day.

Yes, my anger was most certainly growing, and while she laughed and teased with me, it was becoming increasingly difficult to keep my mouth shut. I wanted to scream at her and ask her why she chose this instead of me.

Had she not heard delightful things about me? Did my men not sing praises of my generosity? Was my palace not as large as she had hoped? Did she suspect I was ugly? Was there one reason or were there many?

No matter how many questions I asked myself, how many thoughts ran through my mind, I wouldn't receive any answers sitting here with her. Sure, I could ask her outright, but given I was the man she seemed to be hiding from, there was very little chance of her being open.

And so, I continued to sit in the fields with her for the rest of the week. If she noticed my silence, she did not comment on it; if anything, it made her more talkative.

As the last night before the week changed came, she bid me goodnight, her hand brushing mine. I grasped it for a moment, and she looked up at me with hopeful eyes as I raised it before me, looking down at it.

I longed to break this silence and ask for the truth from her. I longed for something to give. This obvious attraction between us couldn't be ignored for much longer, and it was so tempting to speak. I was sure she felt the same way about me, even if she seemed to brush it off.

There was so much I wanted to say—words I longed to have pouring out of me, baring my heart to her. With this mix of anger, passion, and hope, I just had to find the right words and then I could finally say something.

But before I could, it hit me, like an icy gust in the middle of a blizzard.

The man she was looking at with such eyes, he was a goose boy. He was someone who had nothing and may never have land to call his own. He was someone who could offer her nothing, yet she had endeared herself to him. He was someone else.

Not a king with a throne and all the riches in the world. Not someone who could quite literally offer her all the treasures she could possibly desire, who could spoil her, shower her with gifts, ensure she would want for nothing.

She had fallen for a mere goose boy, and it was in that moment I realized something.

I was afraid.

Because in all this time we had spent together, in the time she had lived in my kingdom, she had not chosen a king. She had not chosen me.

She had chosen Alion.

And it was a realization that shook me to my core. I thought I was the only one giving something in this match of marriage; I thought I had given the better part of this deal. And yet, this realization threatened everything I had believed about royalty and power. I had won a woman over with only my heart to recommend me, and she had accepted me the way I was.

With those thoughts washing over me, I raised her hand to my lips, pressing a gentle kiss to it. Her eyes glowed, and I felt my heart leap. This was what love did to someone... this was what love could do to me.

And all it had taken was two poor royals finding riches in a field of geese.

Chapter Twenty-Three

Catalina

I t took us a week to find some sort of rhythm. I would bring my bag of biscuits and find treats from Alec hidden throughout—treats I would then offer to share with Alion. Alion would bring some ham and cheese scones, cherry pastries, and rich sweet cider. I never questioned where he gathered such royal fare from, but I sure enjoyed more than my fair share.

"I must say, I do appreciate a woman with a hearty appetite." I felt my cheeks turn red as he laughed in that charming way he always did. "Oh, don't be embarrassed. I'm being completely honest."

I wondered whether he would withdraw after such a statement, as he always did, but he didn't this time. I didn't want to read too much into it, as I didn't want to set myself up for disappointment, but it was hard not to.

He was kind, handsome, funny, and smart—everything I would like to imagine in my future. Yet, there was, of course, that nagging voice in the back of my mind reminding me that I was already spoken for, that I was a princess bound to a king.

Still, sometimes there were moments when I enjoyed pretending to be just a simple goose girl. I could smile and flirt with the commoner I worked with. I pretended we would have a wedding in the village square one day and dance as musicians wrote melodies inspired by our love for one another.

Oh boy, I was too far gone. I couldn't allow this to go on for much longer. It was getting harder with each passing day. A village wedding was really not in my future and nothing I did could ever make one happen. It was not who I was set up to be; I was Princess Catalina, the soon-to-be queen of Whyst, and Alion was a farm boy.

I wanted to pull back like he often did, but I was not that sort of person anymore. There was a time when I would have been careful and cautious, but I couldn't do it now, not when I felt so many things and wanted to embrace all of them.

Alion chose that moment to lean over and brush his hand across my cheek, pulling away with what remained of my cherry pastry on his fingers. My palace manners seemed to have disappeared in my time here, and I would have been ashamed, except I was too aware of the feeling his hand left on my skin.

My pulse was dancing and my eyes locked in place as his gazed into mine. It felt as though we had frozen in time and I was scared to move. I couldn't risk him withdrawing again. I wanted this moment to last, as it may be all I had for my future.

"Lia..." he whispered softly. He was so close to me, I was tempted to lean in, but I didn't. I couldn't. "Would you mind if I..." His voice trailed off and my eyes widened, eager to hear his request. He swayed toward me for a moment, but then suddenly, he cleared his throat, reached over me, and grabbed the last scone. "Would you mind if I ate this?"

Slowly nodding, I blinked at him in confusion. That was not where I saw that moment ending. I really needed to get a better handle on myself. We were very clearly not on the same page. He likely wanted to enjoy a mutual friendship, and here I was, fawning all over him.

"Actually, that's not what I wanted." He dropped the scone on the ground and before I knew it, his hand was holding mine and pulling me to my feet. "I don't know what to say and I'm not sure what to do, but that's not what I wanted at all."

"Alion—" But before I could say more, he cut me off and took what little breath I'd managed to breathe in these last minutes.

We went from being steps apart to me being taken into his arms as his lips pressed against mine. I was flying, I was soaring, I was reaching, I was everything in between. I closed my eyes, wanting to drown in his kiss.

He pulled away before I was ready and stared at me for a few seconds. I knew he was going to apologize; I knew he was going to say something that would ruin this incredible moment for me. So, without even thinking, I reached up, grabbed his tunic, and brought his face to mine once more.

I knew it was so wrong given my situation, but I couldn't deny what I wanted and, for once, I just wanted some part of my life to feel real. So I reached a hand up to run through his hair, pushing the hat that always flew across the fields to the ground. I never wanted this moment to end. It was everything I could have imagined it being and so much more.

Everything in my heart was singing as he kissed me with a passion I hadn't expected. We were melting into each other and this was as far as I knew things could go, despite any desire we had to stay in this moment.

It was my turn to bring distance between us, and as we stood there catching our breath, it took all of me to remain calm. Was I supposed to speak after such a moment? Did others discuss these things? Was it to fade into oblivion as quickly as it had arrived? There was so much I didn't know, so many things I had never experienced before, and they were all things I now wanted to experience with Alion.

"Lia, I..." His voice was low, and I wanted to melt when he said my name. "You can't imagine how long..." Suddenly, without warning, he jumped away. There was a flush on his cheeks as he avoided my gaze. "Forgive me, I feel as though we may have... that is..."

I closed my eyes for a split second, trying not to give into the embarrassment I felt. I was soaring a moment ago and now I was crash landing.

"Oh, I mean, it was enjoyable," he added. "I just... I need to go."

I started and finally met his gaze. "Go? Alion, it's the middle of the day. We still have—"

"I'm leaving," he said abruptly, leaning over and stuffing the remainder of our meal into his satchel. "It's nothing. I just need to go."

"Wait, do we need to talk?" I questioned, knowing he likely wouldn't speak about what he was feeling at all. Up until this moment, he'd been a closed book. All I had to go on were gestures and the occasional flirtations.

"No," was his retort. "Talking won't be necessary." He looked up at me, his face softening when he saw my hurt expression. "I just need to take care of something."

"Right now?" I couldn't stop myself from asking. "Is it really something that can only be taken care of now, or are you running away from me?"

"Lia," he breathed out in frustration.

"Don't *Lia* me," I snapped. "Tell me why you're always pulling away from me. Why won't you enjoy our time together? Why can't you relax and just be with me? I know how you feel."

"You know how I feel?" he asked in an accusatory voice. "Trust me, you have no idea how I feel. You have no idea about anything."

Tears filled my vision and I couldn't stop one from falling. He began to lean closer, raising a hand as though to brush it away-before dropping it to his side. "I'm sorry, Lia. I truly am. I just can't be who you need me to be right now."

Before I knew it, I was standing in the field alone, wondering how we'd reached this point. How could I go from flying to falling in mere seconds?

Chapter Twenty-Four

Falco

Pacing did nothing to ease the tension in my body as I considered what had happened between Lia and me today. I was frustrated beyond belief, and I needed to think through some things before meeting with Enrich.

His visit had definitely become public knowledge, as the fake princess had claimed to have some contagious illness that confined her to her rooms. If we didn't already know her identity, this would have added to our suspicions, as the true princess was known to be very close with her family. She would have welcomed a visit with open arms.

My feelings for Lia, for Catalina, had certainly grown in the time we had spent together. And somehow, the real Grendy never questioned my whereabouts during the day. Perhaps she thought I was busy with work.

The question I asked myself was almost too confusing for my mind to wrap around. Was I being unfaithful to Grendy by meeting with Lia? Or was it okay since Grendy was technically supposed to be Lia? Seeing as how I was engaged to Princess Catalina, was it wrong seeing as how Grendy was standing in for Catalina? Or did that make it okay?

I groaned as I sat at the desk in my room, dropping my head into my hands. I could definitely feel a headache coming on.

I couldn't stop thinking as I pondered what that meant for Catalina. After all, she was the one technically being unfaithful. But was she, if the person she was being unfaithful with was me? Normally, I couldn't condone such behaviour, but I had also lied about my identity. I wondered if she was having her own struggles, knowing how she felt about Alion while being engaged to King Falco, yet not knowing they were the same person.

Should I be angry with her about that? I definitely felt like some of my resentment toward her was rooted in her ability to just throw away a kingdom and a king. She had wonderful characteristics and was clearly the kind of woman who was perfect for running a kingdom, but we were simply not on the same page.

She enjoyed the simplicity of the fields, and I could never wait to get back to my life at the castle. My only wish was that I could bring her with me and combine the joy of being with her and the joy of being in my home.

Oh, what had I done? I'd intended to get to know Lia in a field and figure out why she was there. I'd never expected to feel attracted to her and to have that attraction be mutual. I never expected that I would be struggling with these things.

I was a king; I was king to one of the most powerful nations in the realms. I could give her everything, I could be everything for her. So why had she chosen to spend her days sitting in a field instead of sitting by my side?

There was one thing I knew for certain; I was in trouble and I needed to find Enrich.

Chapter Twenty-Five

Catalina

Alion didn't show up in the fields the following morning. I waited under the tree where we'd grown accustomed to meeting before continuing our day, but he was nowhere to be seen. Noon came and went without a sign of him. All day I held out hope, but by the time the sun was setting, I knew he wasn't coming. Given how we'd parted the day before, I wasn't sure whether to feel happy, sad, or frustrated.

On one hand, I had my engagement to think of—something I should consider more seriously. I'd kissed another man while being engaged to someone. It didn't matter that I'd never met my betrothed or that I had feelings for the man I actually knew. I'd made a commitment and without even knowing my betrothed, I'd betrayed that commitment.

On the other hand, Alion was present. He was here; he wasn't just someone who lived in the castle on the hill behind us, someone who only cared about marrying a princess. Alion was a man I'd met on a ship and then reunited on a field. There was something special about that. There was no comparison of riches or rankings, there was just us.

Granted, he had no idea who I truly was, and once he found out, he may very well leave me. Not to mention I felt guilty. No matter how I tried to justify what I was doing, the guilt remained.

"Something troubling you, dearie?"

I startled and found myself gazing at a peculiar woman. Normally, when I walked these grounds at night, there was no one but myself wandering around. She had long hair that blew in the wind and her dress was a colour I couldn't quite describe, shimmering somewhere between purple and blue. She looked so out of place.

"Laelynn," she gestured to herself. "And you are?"

That was an excellent question. Who exactly was I? "Ah... Lia." I figured as long as I worked for Alec, I'd best be Lia. Less confusion that way.

"Well Lia, I hate to give you the shoe, but you're on private property here. Oh, sure, some gander through here when they need to get somewhere, but we don't much like folks to dawdle."

Suddenly, it hit me. "You must be the sister Alec had mentioned to me when I first started!" I was far too excited to meet her, but I couldn't help it. In the time I'd stayed with Alec, he'd told me such endearing stories about her. She was flighty as a bird, yet as reliable as they came. He spoke of her so often, I felt like I knew her already.

"Are you someone my brother hired, then?" She lifted a brow and looked me up and down. "You're not the sort I'd have thought would work with geese."

My heart beat a little faster at her words. What was she meaning by that? I didn't need to ask out loud before she nodded at me with a smile.

"I only mean you look a bit soft for geese work. Those birds could bite your head clean off if you're not careful."

A laugh escaped me with her words. "I can't argue with that. There are some truly sassy ones in this flock. I may have threatened some that they may become dinner."

"So you can manage yourself well, I take it." Her voice held a captivating note in it as she spoke with such expressive joy. "But tell me, what brings you out here so close to midnight? For myself, I'm known to stroll here whenever I return home, but you've got a certain look about you... a pensive one."

I'm not sure I liked being read so easily, but there was a welcoming feeling around Laelynn that one couldn't help but resist. "You wouldn't believe me if I told you."

A quick wink was all she gave me, as if to say, "Try me."

"I can't give you all the details," I started with a sigh, "but basically I'm engaged to a man I've never met, and I'm to marry him at the end of this week. But I've gone and fallen for someone else. Someone who I think wants me, but is so back and forth, I haven't got a grasp of it yet."

"Oh dear…" The way her voice trailed off reminded me of Grendy, and I smiled. "So you're not sure what to do?"

"Well, I know what I'm *supposed* to do, but it's not exactly what I *want* to do. You see where I have trouble?"

"Indeed." She plopped down onto the grass unceremoniously and rested her head atop her knees. She was remarkably spry for her age. "And what will you actually do?"

"I'm not sure yet. I feel like I keep running away from where everyone is telling me to go. Being here, working here, it's the first time I was able to be completely on my own, and even this was something that was set up for me by someone else."

Laelynn watched me for a few minutes before she finally spoke. "When you run from destiny, it finds you, but never on your terms. When you take control and seek your own destiny, things have a way of working out, because you embraced the power of choosing for yourself."

"But that doesn't make any sense." She only added to my confusion when she spoke, and it was as though her words contradicted my experiences. "I haven't been able to seek my own destiny because everyone else is too busy trying to tell me what it is."

"Have they been telling it to you or have you just been avoiding it by making excuses for yourself? You say others have chosen everything, but then you ended up in a field talking to an old lady."

"I would like to make other choices, though. I had to make this one in secret." I was growing frustrated with her. I know it was pointless, but I was. "It's true I'm here of my own choosing, but I don't get to choose to continue on here. I have to return to where I'm bound, fulfill someone else's destiny."

Laelynn shook her head. "Dearie, it's not possible to fulfil someone else's destiny. It is only possible to meet your own. But it is up to you to decide. Have you met your own yet? Or has your journey been extended?"

I closed my eyes for a moment and took a deep breath. "I don't know... How will I know?"

"You will know."

When I opened my eyes, she was gone.

Chapter Twenty-Six

Catalina

I listened to Alec and Laelynn banter as I packed my breakfast that morning. You would think they were children the way they went about it, yet the repeated comments of one's old age made it very clear they were not.

I made a sound with my throat to capture their attention and they both glanced up at me. "I know this is sudden notice, but unfortunately, I'll not be able to continue working here for much longer."

Neither of them looked surprised. Laelynn gave a smile, and Alec nodded thoughtfully. He spoke up first. "Will you visit then, for tea when it suits?"

Oh, I would miss him so much. He'd become like a darling grandfather to me in our short time together, and I wish I could have spent more time here. Would he want me visiting if he knew who I was? If he knew I wasn't truly Lia?

"I would like that very much if you still want me to." I looked away awkwardly. "You see, I'm not exactly who I said I was..."

"Well, of course you're not," he grunted. "We may live in the countryside, but we don't need a palace education to know you're not from around here."

His words startled me, but I should have expected them. My manners, my way of speaking, even the clothing Grendy and I had packed, all showed this wasn't my usual lifestyle.

"You work hard and you've a good head on your shoulders. I'll miss having you around, but my flighty sister will keep me company here for now."

Laelynn let out a tinkling laugh as she ruffled his head. "Who are you calling flighty?"

I took the bag I'd packed that morning and gave them each a quick hug, promising to visit as soon as I could. I made a note in my head to deliver an invitation to the wedding the next time I was here. Surely, I could invite the few friends I'd made here in Whyst.

Except, of course, for Alion.

Chapter Twenty-Seven

Alion

T he day I had missed with Catalina felt painful. I didn't realize how much I depended on seeing her every single day. It was strange how one could fall for someone so quickly, even stranger, when that person was the one you needed to marry.

I had spent all day with her brother yesterday, going over every single detail. I explained how I'd been spending time in the field she worked in, and Enrich had been furious.

"Am I to believe you've been alone with my sister, running through a field every day for the past week? While her maid avoids me since she suspects I am here, and I've been trapped waiting to hear back from my messengers?"

"Yes, that is exactly the situation. You seem to have a good grasp on it." He glared daggers at me when my good humour showed. I couldn't help it, Catalina had that effect on me these days.

Once he had gotten over his initial big brother moment, we launched into our next plan of action. We would need to act quickly to make this work in our favour. With Catalina and a kingdom in danger, there was no telling what could go wrong if we didn't do this right.

I was practically skipping on my way to the field. It was just past noon, and I hadn't seen her in two days, far longer than I was ever willing to go again. Although it was possible she would be furious once she realized what I had done. And there would likely be confusion with her feelings in regards to both Falco and me, given that we were the same person.

No sooner had I arrived than she looked over at me with a small smile. I knew we hadn't spoken since our kiss and we hadn't parted on the best of terms, but I wasn't expecting to see her so forlorn.

I started to greet her, but she held up her hand. "Alion," she started. "This is goodbye."

I looked down at the bag she had at her feet and with a start, I realized what was happening. She was leaving now, this instant, before I had a chance to explain myself. This meant she was either heading off on a new adventure or she was heading to the palace. If the first, I would lose track of her and Enrich would be justifiably angry at me for messing all this up. If the second, she would learn quite quickly that I was King Falco.

This wasn't good.

"Don't go yet. I really need to talk to you."

"It'd be best if we didn't." She avoided my gaze as she hoisted her bag over her shoulder.

I reached out a hand to grasp her arm gently. "Please. It can't wait." I knew my voice sounded desperate, but I couldn't help it. I felt like I was losing her.

"I know there are things we haven't talked about, and maybe we'll never talk about those things, but trust me when I tell you, this is for the best." Her words confused me, even though I knew our situation more clearly than she did.

"Where are you going? How will I find you?" I had to know.

She took the hand that held her arm. "This time with you has felt special to me, and I know it's the same for you, but there's a back and forth between us. I don't know why it exists on your end, but I know why it exists on mine, and it's time for me to acknowledge that and move on. There's something I've been committed to for some time, and I need to honour that."

She was choosing Falco. Relief filled my body, but then I froze. No, I couldn't feel relief right now. As soon as she would step foot in those doors and be greeted by King Falco, by myself, she would be furious. This had gone wrong so quickly. Nothing was ever easy as a king.

"You can't go yet."

Something in my voice must have convinced her, because she stopped and gave me a strange look.

"And why not?"

Without thinking, I grabbed her and pulled her to my body. The bag on her shoulder fell awkwardly from its place and my lips found hers. We'd been in this position two days ago, yet it felt like a brand-new sensation as I kissed her.

I didn't know what I was hoping to do. For a moment, I thought I could buy more time to really think things through, but I hadn't realized that kissing her would wipe all sound logic from my mind. I felt her melt into our kiss, and my heart lifted when I realized I hadn't messed this up.

She pulled back and we stood close to each other for a few minutes, catching our breath. Our eyes were caught on one another and she lifted a hand to cup my cheek. Her smile was sad as she took a step away from me. "Goodbye, Alion."

I tried to regain my composure, but it was no use. She walked away. My rash behaviour had cost me the only chance I would have at convincing her to stay just one more day. I could kick myself. What was I going to tell Enrich?

Chapter Twenty-Eight

Grendy

There were strange happenings about as I snuck down the corridor with a hood pulled over my head. So far, I'd been pleased with how things were unfolding as I considered my plans, but there was something that had been amiss for the last week.

Falco had stopped displaying any interest in me, regarding me with cold, unfeeling eyes. It played right into my plans, yet there was a measure of guilt I felt at the deception Catalina and I had begun.

Catalina was the warmest and dearest person I had ever had the pleasure of knowing, and that complicated the current situation in a way I had never expected. It made me feel regret, and I almost resented her for that. Of course, one could never resent Catalina. When I first started as her maid, I felt much resentment, but that had faded over time. Thankfully and unfortunately.

Brushing aside my thoughts, I continued down the hall, ducking into darkened doorways when I heard any threat of being discovered.

King Enrich had shown up. No one knew that I knew, but I certainly did. He was hidden away as a surprise for my wedding day, but he had no idea I was really Grendy. And how could he know when our paths had yet to cross?

I was suspicious of him showing up. He'd left his mother and primary adviser behind in order to attend a royal wedding in a different land? It didn't seem right in my mind. There was something dishonest going on, other than Catalina and my plans. The anxiety was taking over, and it was painful not knowing what was happening behind closed doors.

I finally escaped the castle after dodging everyone I possibly could and took a deep breath. Out here, one could truly breathe. I didn't know how anyone could tolerate living in a place of this size. Catalina's home had somehow been warm and inviting—a place locals loved to travel to and experience. Their grounds were always open to the public, and the wall was merely a defense against crimes.

Whyst was different. It was a land that boasted a large army, a growing harbour, plenty of resources, a full treasury, and even the capital city alone had a bigger population than the whole of Maryn. King Falco was generous with his coffers but still, he was frivolous as well. It was infuriating.

As I approached the field before me, I saw Catalina in the distance. It was later than we usually met, but she appeared to be holding a large bag—the travel bag we had filled on the ship. A foreboding feeling washed over me and I knew this couldn't be good.

"Grendy, I'm so glad you came. I wasn't sure if you would," she started excitedly. "I've decided I'll walk back with you tonight so we can go about undoing our small amusement."

She was unusually chipper, a welcome change from her quiet mood of late, but there was something about her I couldn't read.

"Has something brought on this decision? I thought we might discuss this for a length of time before suddenly having you appear. Won't that be strange to everyone?"

Catalina hesitated, and her bag slowly dropped to the ground. "Why, I'm sure it would be. But you and I always knew that would happen. I've given notice to the farmer who resides here, as well as the man I worked with, and it's time to move on."

My heart startled. The man she worked with? When I had secured this place for her, I was assured she would be completely alone, isolated. With no one to connect with other than an elderly man who ran the farm. It was the only way I could ensure our plan would remain intact.

"What man?" I asked abruptly. "What man did you work with?"

"Well, I never told you, and I'm not sure why, but do you remember one of the ship hands? He wasn't my usual sort, but he was so kind. We spent a lot of time together..."

Her voice faded as my mind sharpened suddenly. Surely, she couldn't mean... It wasn't possible. There was no way Falco had found her here. A roaring sound filled my ears as blood rushed to my head. It couldn't be.

"Grendy?" Catalina's voice called me back into focus, and I narrowed my eyes as her next words came. "You remember him, right? His name was Alion?"

While I had been sitting in the castle all this time, it seemed Falco had his own agenda and was meeting Catalina in this very spot.

My heart began to pound as panic set in. Did he know she was the princess? Or was he, like Catalina, merely into the idea of finding simplicity and enjoying a different life? Had he fallen for Catalina on the ship without realizing she was the true princess?

There were so many questions, yet all of them remained unanswered. I couldn't very well tell her he was the king, but I also couldn't have her return to the castle and figure it out for herself. Everything I did depended on this very moment.

Throwing everything to the wind, I took a step toward her.

"Princess, you'll need to come with me."

Chapter Twenty-Nine

Falco

Enrich's messenger had returned at a completely indecent hour, so it was shortly before midnight when I was awakened by a large knock on the door.

"Falco, it's me."

I could hear my guards try to calm Enrich on the other side, but there was an edge to his voice I couldn't ignore. Flinging the door open, I glared at him. "Can this not wait until morning?"

"It certainly cannot," he huffed, uncharacteristically out of sorts. "You must come with me. Immediately. Summon a full guard."

I closed the door in his face, much to his displeasure, as he continued to knock. "At least wait there until I'm dressed in more than a robe, Enrich. You must afford me that comfort." A few minutes later, I strode out to a rather annoyed king, fully dressed, with a sword at my side and a knife in my belt.

He eyed the weapons and gave a slight nod of approval. "I'll fill you in as we go, but we must make haste. The news I received was not good."

"Worse than your sister trading places to get away from me?"

"You're not still upset about that, are you? Besides, you don't know if that's the reason."

I rolled my eyes as I tried to keep up with his quickening pace. "And what other reason could there be? You made quite sure she wouldn't find out about anything happening around her."

He halted for a split second before rushing ahead again. "You disapprove of my tactics?" He waved his hand at the guards who joined us, these ones wearing his colours. I had no idea when they had arrived, but he'd done his diligence. "When you have a daughter, you will understand."

"A daughter? Catalina is your sister."

"I have cared for her like a daughter since our father passed. In this moment, she is more my daughter than my sister. And until she is married to you, I will protect her."

"Do you not think she can protect herself?"

"Falco, do not test me. She is a capable woman, but she doesn't have the experience to protect herself."

His answer angered me. He barely even saw Catalina as someone who could fend for herself. I knew she came from a specific way of life, but she knew who she was and she stood firm in that. I'd seen her scare coyotes and more away from the geese we had tended. She was fierce when the occasion called for it.

"Where are we rushing off to, Enrich?"

"We need to head to that field and find Catalina."

I caught his arm just as we were exiting the front gate. "Catalina won't be there. She intends to make her way to the castle. I tried finding you earlier so I could tell you, but you were nowhere to be seen."

"What do you mean?" His eyes were dark as they looked into mine. "It is not safe here. Not with—" He spun around, foul words leaving his mouth.

"With what? Enrich, please, you must inform me of what is happening."

He didn't stop, and I was forced to chase after him. No matter how much I asked, he didn't turn to continue the conversation. He pushed forward with an intensity that was alarming. Whatever he had learned, it wasn't good.

When we finally did stop, we were outside Alec's cottage and everything around us was dark. It was around two in the morning, and I was feeling apologetic about disturbing the elderly farmer.

"How did you know where to find this place?"

He gave me a look and commented, "You really think I would have seen my sister working for a farmer and not immediately found out the location at which she was staying?"

"Ah, good point."

He raised a hand to knock and my own shot up to grab his. Gesturing to be quiet with my free hand, I paused for a moment. There were voices inside.

Why would there be voices at this hour?

Chapter Thirty

Catalina

G rendy had taken me right back to Alec's place, and I had
no idea why. She'd instructed I hide in the cellar and for
some reason, I'd followed her directions. Now, as I pushed up
against the door, I found myself trapped.

"Grendy! You have to let me out and tell me what's going on."

"Not now." Her calm voice came through in response. "All is
well."

All was clearly not well. I was trapped in a cellar in the middle
of the night, and I had no idea what Grendy was thinking. I
heard her speaking with Alec in a sharp tone and his soft words
in response. Was she giving away my identity right now?

I saw a faint glimpse of moonlight streaming in across the
room—a cellar door leading outside. If I could find my way to
open it in the dark, I could escape and figure out what was going
on.

Escape? What was I thinking? That would imply that I had been captured, and surely, this was just a safety precaution that Grendy was taking.

The door above me opened and Grendy stuck her hand down. "Here, princess," she whispered. "A drink to keep you comfortable. I will share in due time."

I took the mug she offered me and smelled the sweet tea that occupied it. A warning bell went off at the strangeness of this moment, but surely, I was safe. After all, Grendy took the very best care of me. "Thank you," was all I said as I accepted it, taking a sip to satisfy her.

As soon as the door above me was locked, I put the mug down and rushed across the cellar. I wasn't sticking around here to find out what all these strange happenings were. Grendy was rousing more suspicion with each passing moment. Something wasn't right here.

The old Catalina would have sat and waited until someone came to fetch her, but having found my independence, I was no longer content to sit and wait.

Picking up a tool I tripped over on the way, I stumbled to the cellar door. Fumbling around for the handle and the lock that was closed over it, I pried it open with everything I could, but it didn't budge. Positioning myself to place my body weight on the tool I carried, I pressed as hard as I could.

A snapping sound echoed and for a moment, I was worried I'd broken the tool, but thankfully, the lock shattered under my weight and I was able to unlatch it.

"A few too many sweets in my time here in Whyst," I mumbled to myself. "I would benefit greatly from a vegetable."

I climbed the short ladder to the ground level and turned quickly to ensure no one had seen my escape. I still had my bag with me, thankfully, and there wasn't anything I needed. My head clouded and I swayed, suddenly unsteady on my feet. What was the matter with me?

I snuck around the corner to the front of the cottage, only to pull back quickly at what I saw. Two men and a full detail ten paces behind them, all waiting outside the door. This wasn't good. Something was happening here and for the first time, I felt frightened.

The world around me became hazy and my stomach lurched. More alarm bells sounded and without another step, I felt my body sink to the ground with a *thud*.

The tea… I thought with a start. The tea Grendy had given me. Had she poisoned me? No, that couldn't be. Was I going mental? She would never do a thing like that. She was my maid.

The two figures in front of the door spun as these thoughts fluttered in and out. Before I could make out either of their faces, the world went dark.

"Catalina!" a voice called through the haze.

And then, nothing.

Chapter Thirty-One

Falco

Everything happened at once and I could barely keep up.

Catalina appeared from nowhere around the back of the cottage, then collapsed. The guard detail lurched closer, out of alarm for our safety. The front door flew open to reveal a shocked Grendy. And then chaos ensued.

"Get Catalina!" Enrich called over the commotion as he lunged forward to grab Grendy, barely managing to grasp her hair and yank her back. Grendy pulled away from Enrich and, much to my surprise, I saw her grab Catalina, lift her up in her unconscious state, and spin around to face everyone, a dagger inches from Catalina's face. "One more step," she threatened.

"Stop!" I called out to the guards.

Grendy wore a sneer as she took in her surroundings. Her odds were slim, but she had managed to bargain with the one person she knew no one could do without. The person who held the fate of her home in her hands.

"Who are you?" I demanded.

"Just a lowly maid," she snapped. "No need to concern yourself with more than that."

"Who are you really?" I questioned again. "Wouldn't you rather your grand deception be credited to you at the end of all this?"

She considered my questions, and then a sly smile slid across her face. She balanced Catalina between her arms, adjusting her stance to account for the full weight of the form I hoped was only sleeping.

Taking a step, Enrich pushed forward. "What did you do to her?"

"Not another boot should move closer to me, king," she snarled. "A mere sedative to prevent an escape that I supposed she'd be bold enough to take. A mug that should knock her out for a day, at least."

"Why did you do this? Why would you take her place?" I would finally get the answer I sought. I would finally know why Catalina avoided the king of Whyst.

"It was her idea. She made this all too easy. My job was to get rid of her, but sticking her in a field and slowly taking away her right to the crown made it all too easy."

"I knew it was you," Enrich snapped. "As soon as my messenger told me there was a traitor, I knew it was you." I could see him fighting back the urge to move, and Grendy pressed the knife along Catalina's neck, a small drop of blood appearing under.

"Yes, and I've got nothing to lose now that my job will be complete. Catalina won't be able to save her precious home and there will be no marital union. All has fallen into place more perfectly than I could have imagined."

"Why?" I asked. "Why did you do this?"

"Because," she spat out, "you rich royals are all the same. You build your stained-glass palaces and bribe your ship men. You seek to control and add to your treasuries with no thought of those beneath you."

"Grendy…" Enrich whispered. "Did we not take you in as one of our own? We knew you hailed from Zenyth, yet we took you in. Despite their rebellions, despite their coups."

"You did. And look where your naivety landed you, king." She nodded her head around. "A failed betrothal and a soon-to-be dead princess." With a final sneer, she pulled her hand back, ready to drive the tip of the dagger home.

Before anyone could move, a loud clang could be heard and the expression on Grendy's face froze. Time stood still for a moment, then her body crumpled next to Catalina's. Everyone blinked in shock, no one daring to move, until we looked at the figure standing directly behind her, a shovel raised in the air.

"She never accepted the tea I offered her," Alec mumbled in annoyance. "I knew she was bad news right then."

Chapter Thirty-Two

Catalina

W here I awoke was certainly not the same place in which I had fallen. I blinked back the blurriness as I glanced around the room. A soft mattress was under me, large billowing curtains around me, and tapestries lined the walls. I wasn't in the cottage anymore, that was for certain.

I bolted upright, groaning at the feeling that came over my head in the rush. Pressing my hands to my temple, I tried to remember everything I could. I'd planned on rushing to the castle and then stumbled across two men and a party of guards. One of them had a strangely familiar voice.

"You're awake," the familiar voice cried out.

I jumped and turned to face him. "Enrich?" It was my brother. I pinched my skin in an effort to revive myself, but it was him sitting beside the bed. "What on earth are you doing here?"

"Lina," was all he said as he leaned forward and gathered me into his arms. "Oh, Lina!"

There were very few times I'd seen my brother get emotional, and while I would have loved to treasure this show of affection, I was more confused than ever.

The door to the chamber swung open and through the haze of my vision, which was still clearing, I saw someone enter, along with a siege of maids and footmen. My confusion grew. Was I hallucinating?

The figure stopped before the bed and I realized something.

"A-Alion?" I stammered, slowly climbing to my feet, steadying myself with one hand on the bedpost at the foot of the bed. "Is that you?"

"It's Falco, actually," he returned, smiling at me.

Falco... This was... No, it couldn't be. This was Alion. Falco was a king... the king of Whyst. This man before me couldn't be Falco.

"No," I began, "you're Alion. The goose boy."

Enrich glanced between us as we stood locked on one another before raising himself up and making his way to the door. "It seems you have things to discuss. I will see if the arrangements for Grendy's keep are up to standard."

Neither of us turned to look at him and the comment made about Grendy did not even phase me. I had likely misheard, and either way, I would see to that later.

The silence that stretched between us was awkward as it seemed neither of us wanted to speak first. That was fine by me; I could be stubborn. I raised an eyebrow, and he finally chuckled. "I suppose I can explain."

"Yes," I replied coolly. "I suppose you could."

"I'm King Falco."

"Yes, I'd gathered."

A nervous laugh escaped him and I turned away from him to pace, which was the best way to hear his explanation and prevent unleashing my frustrations onto him.

"You see, you were coming here to marry me, but I didn't know who you were," he started. "I didn't want to marry a complete stranger, so I thought I might hide on the ship and get to know you there."

I stopped my walking. "But the men—"

"I bribed them."

"Of course." I rolled my eyes, then continued spinning around to face him.

"But while I thought I was watching the princess and getting to know her—"

"You were really watching Grendy."

"Ah... Correct. Because you had traded places."

"And how did you find the princess before you knew these facts?" I couldn't resist asking. He'd spent nearly two weeks in Grendy's company. The wedding was to take place tomorrow, if it was even still happening. What had he been doing with her in this castle?

"She was... disappointing."

My eyes raised to meet his, and I couldn't hide the pleasure I'd found in that statement. "Truly?"

Alion, no, Falco took a step toward me. "Truly." I couldn't move as he continued, "And the entire time I was with her, I couldn't stop thinking about her maid."

"Her maid?" I knew my expression betrayed me.

"Her maid," he confirmed with another step. "I tried to force myself to forget this maid until one night when everything changed..."

"What changed?" I probed.

"Her brother and I followed the princess to a field, where it was revealed to me that I was not with the princess after all. That the woman I was set to marry was none other than the very maid I could not keep from my mind."

"Oh," I breathed, unsure of what else to say. Was he telling me what I had been longing to hear all week? Where was the anger at being betrayed? Should I feel the same anger with him for hiding his identity? Were we actually on even ground? Finally?

The distance between us finally closed and he stood, looked down at me, his eyes communicating so much more than I had expected.

"I'm sorry," I spoke, "for deceiving you, for all of this—"

His lips met mine briefly, cutting off the words I'd intended to say. "For doing the same thing I intended to do right from the start? For wanting to know the person you're betrothed to marry?"

"I suppose so..."

"Lia, you fell for me in a place no one else would."

"Hold on," I fought, looking for anything firm to stand upon before this man would whisk me away too far. "What makes you think I fell for you?"

"I don't see you pulling away from me," he pointed out as his arms wrapped around me, holding me to him.

He was correct, but still... "I was unfaithful to the man I was supposed to marry." A topic that surely would have come up later.

"It was me the whole time," he reminded me, lightheartedly.

"You know what I look like with goose droppings on my cheek."

Falco let out a laugh and tightened his grip around me for a moment before falling to his knee. He looked up at me with a smile on his face, his eyes twinkling, and I knew what was coming.

"Lia, princess of the goose fields and the wind whisperer of hats, will you marry me tomorrow?"

Epilogue

The wedding that had been planned was somehow redone overnight. Gone was the giant cake in the marble hall and elaborate decorations. Gone was the long train for my dress and the dressing gown for Falco. Gone was it all.

For when I'd sat in his arms looking out at the stars on our first night as ourselves and our last unmarried night, I'd shared my secret dream of a wedding in a village square with cookies, pies, and cakes. A pig on to roast, and the village girls dancing with flower crowns adorning their head. Men bragging about their latest ocean catch, and women showing off their special occasion dresses.

And who should be there in the middle of it all but Alec and Laelynn, there to join in the merriment of it all.

"I knew you were no ordinary goose girl," Alec said with a wink. "And that one was certainly the king when he showed up at my door. But I know when to keep my mouth shut, I sure do."

It was a beautiful occasion, open to all who would attend. The first of many occasions with royals and villagers alike. And as I danced on Falco's arms, being twirled lovingly in his arms, I knew this was going to be a day I would live over again in my mind.

The perfect wedding.

Of course, no one knew what to make of our tale when it all did finally come out. We were a strange couple, always referring to each other by the wrong names and laughing when no one could follow along with what was happening.

Yet we fit. We fit together in a way no one could understand. It wasn't our titles that bound us together or the betrothal document that had been signed what felt like ages ago; it was the bond we had created on a ship, in a field, in each other's arms. We were bound to one another in a way that was beyond what anyone could grasp.

And so, I had found what I always longed for in days gone by. A love so unique, so deep, that no one could deny it.

And all it had taken was a deceptive maid, some wayward geese, and a whole lot of pastries.

The End

Join the Fight

"The only thing necessary for the triumph of evil is for good people to do nothing."
— Edmund Burke

The purpose of the Hope Ever After series is to spread hope and be an avenue to support and raise awareness in the fight against human trafficking and slavery.

The trafficking industry is estimated to generate roughly $150 billion a year and is the fastest growing form of international crime, according to UNICEF. Every thirty seconds, another person becomes a trafficking victim.

How can you help?

Educate yourself on how to recognize a victim of trafficking.

Pray. Pray for victims, and pray for those in the operations who are searching for and rescuing victims.

Buy all the books in the Hope Ever After series! All the proceeds from this series go to the O.U.R. to fight and end sex trafficking.

We hope our books inspire you to join the fight against human trafficking because God's children are not for sale. Thank you so much for your support!

Hope Ever After

Hope Ever After is a collection of twenty hopeful and uplifting fairy tale retellings.

Each book is written by a different author and can be enjoyed in any order. The proceeds from this series are donated to the O.U.R. (Operation Underground Rescue) to rescue children from exploitation and trafficking.

Be sure to collect all twenty, as the entire series, put together, forms a rainbow, a symbol of hope and of God's love!

An Ambitious Hope: A Red Riding Hood Retelling by Lucy Winton

A Gentle Hope: A Beauty and the Beast Retelling by Sarah Carlisle

A Silent Hope: A Wounded Lion Retelling by Madisyn Carlin

A Fairest Hope: A Snow White Retelling by S. Lee Poole

A Crowned Hope: A Prince and the Pauper Retelling by Kayla Eshbaugh

A Golden Hope: A Rumpelstiltskin Retelling by Chelsey Noelle

A Beautiful Hope: An Ugly Duckling Retelling by Leialoha Humpherys

A Renewed Hope: A Princess and the Pea Retelling by Robyn Sarty

with Poetry by Scarlett Luna Strange and Selina De Luca

A Charming Hope: A Frog Prince Retelling by Ashley Evercott

An Enduring Hope: A Wild Swans Retelling by Jes Drew

A Cascading Hope: A Little Mermaid Retelling by Yakira Goldsberry

A Midnight Hope: A Cinderella Retelling by Stefanie Lozinski

A Faithful Hope: A Blue Bird Retelling by DaLeena Taylor

A Gracious Hope: A Sleeping Beauty Retelling by Robyn Sarty

A Wishful Hope: An Aladdin Retelling by Sarah Beran

A Healing Hope: A Rapunzel Retelling by Selina De Luca

A Wingless Hope: A Thumbelina Retelling by Sydney Winward

A Secret Hope: A Goose Girl Retelling by Scarlett Luna Strange

A Frigid Hope: A Snow Queen Retelling by Amanda Thompson

A Last Hope: A King Thrushbeard Retelling by Verity Sandahl

Find them all at https://books2read.com/rl/HopeEverAfter

About the Author

Scarlett Luna Strange has always been obsessed with reading and writing fantasy stories. After finding success in a different genre, she decided to launch a brand new career with her pen name and explore the world of fantasy. Her debut novel released June 2023 and she hopes to continue writing forever.

She lives in a small town nestled in mountains and spends much of her time exploring the surrounding forests and lakes with her husband and their dog.

https://scarlett-luna-strange.squarespace.com/

my newsletter

find more
books here

instagram

facebook

tiktok

www.ingramcontent.com/pod-product-compliance
Lightning Source LLC
Chambersburg PA
CBHW051944170626
46808CB00007B/2477